Also by Alex Morgan

THE KICKS

Saving the Team

Win or Lose

Hat Trick

Shaken Up

Settle the Score

BREAKAWAY: BEYOND THE GOAL

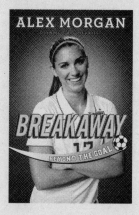

ALEX MORGAN

Simon & Schuster Books for Young Readers
New York   London   Toronto   Sydney   New Delhi

SIMON & SCHUSTER BOOKS FOR YOUNG READERS
An imprint of Simon & Schuster Children's Publishing Division
1230 Avenue of the Americas, New York, New York 10020
This book is a work of fiction. Any references to historical events, real people, or real places are used fictitiously. Other names, characters, places, and events are products of the author's imagination, and any resemblance to actual events or places or persons, living or dead, is entirely coincidental.
Copyright © 2013 by Alex Morgan and Full Fathom Five
All rights reserved, including the right of reproduction in whole or in part in any form.
SIMON & SCHUSTER BOOKS FOR YOUNG READERS is a trademark of Simon & Schuster, Inc.
For information about special discounts for bulk purchases, please contact Simon & Schuster Special Sales at 1-866-506-1949 or business@simonandschuster.com.
The Simon & Schuster Speakers Bureau can bring authors to your live event. For more information or to book an event, contact the Simon & Schuster Speakers Bureau at 1-866-248-3049 or visit our website at www.simonspeakers.com.
Also available in a Simon & Schuster Books for Young Readers hardcover edition
Book design by Krista Vossen
The text for this book is set in Berling.
Manufactured in the United States of America
0516 OFF
First Simon & Schuster Books for Young Readers paperback edition June 2014
6 8 10 9 7
The Library of Congress has cataloged the hardcover edition as follows:
Morgan, Alex (Alexandra Patricia), 1989–
Sabotage season / Alex Morgan. — First edition.
pages cm. — (The Kicks ; [2])
Summary: "Devin and the rest of the team must figure out who is trying to sabotage them before the playoffs start"— Provided by publisher.
ISBN 978-1-4424-8574-7 (hardback) — ISBN 978-1-4424-8576-1 (pbk) —
ISBN 978-1-4424-8578-5 (ebook)
[1. Soccer—Fiction. 2. Friendship—Fiction. 3. Sabotage—Fiction. 4. Family life—California—Fiction. 5. California—Fiction.] I. Title.
PZ7.M818Sab 2013   [Fic]—dc23   2013010894

full
fathom
five

FOR MY CYPRESS ELITE TEAMMATES

AND COACHES SAL, DAVE, AND EDUARDO.

THIS IS WHERE IT ALL BEGAN.

CHAPTER ONE

"Devin? Is that you?"

I set down the huge bag of soccer balls I was carrying and turned to see Coach Flores behind me.

"Hi, Coach," I said. "I thought I'd set up the practice field early, since it's my turn to run practice today."

Coach smiled at me. "Need any help? I was just doing some paperwork in my office when I heard noise in the equipment room, but I can finish up later if you want."

I shook my head. "Thanks, but there's not much to do. I kind of want to get my head ready too. Know what I mean?"

She nodded. "Back in the day, my mom used to bring me to the field an hour before we had to report for each game, but I didn't mind. It helped me to calm down and focus."

"Exactly," I agreed.

Coach headed back to her office, and I carried the balls from the equipment room out to the Kentville Middle School soccer field. I had to admit, I was feeling pretty pumped up. First, the boys' team was at an away game, so we got to use their practice field instead of our crummy field of weeds with garbage cans for goalposts. Second, Coach had said that the team co-captains could each run a practice this week to get leadership experience, and today was my turn. And the third reason was that I had figured out something awesome.

Our team, the Kentville Kangaroos (otherwise known as the Kicks), had a shot at making the play-offs! When I first joined the team, I never thought we had a chance. At the start of the season, we were pretty awful. We lost a bunch of games, but then we figured things out, and we got a lot better. We tied a game, and we even beat the Pinewood Panthers—a really strong team—the second time we played them. And now there was actually a chance—a small one—that we could make the play-offs. I knew if we worked hard, we could keep winning, and that made me happy. As co-captain, it was part of my job to make sure we were the best team we could be.

The afternoon sun shone down on the field, and I admired the perfectly trimmed green grass and the freshly painted white lines. I dumped out the balls and then started dribbling around the circumference of the field, just because I could.

"Hey, Devin! Don't tire yourself out!"

I squinted and saw my friend Jessi walking onto the field. She was the first person I'd made friends with when I'd moved to Kentville a few months before, and in addition to my friend Kara back in Connecticut, Jessi was one of my best friends.

I dribbled up to her. "You're here just in time to help me set up the cones," I said.

She grinned. "Anything for my captain."

"Co-captain," I reminded her. "Anyway, I'm psyched for practice. I stayed up last night looking at some drills online. I've got some new stuff we can try out."

"I don't know. I kind of liked Grace's last practice," Jessi said, mentioning the eighth grader who co-captained the team with me. "Some dribbling, a scrimmage, and then done. Not too stressful."

"Well, I've got some defensive drills for us," I told her. "I know we beat the Panthers last time, but they had way too many scoring attempts in that game. I found a couple of drills that I think are really going to make our blocking and intercepting skills better."

"Whoa, you're totally taking this seriously," Jessi said.

"Well, I found something out," I said. "After we beat the Panthers, I checked the stats in our division. The Panthers and the Vipers are pretty much guaranteed play-off spots. But the third and fourth places are open. If we keep winning, we could get one of those slots."

Jessi raised an eyebrow. "Seriously? The Kicks? In the play-offs?"

I nodded. "It could happen."

Jessi grinned. "Then bring it on!"

"I will," I promised. "Come on. Let's go get those cones."

We set up the cones to form two squares on the field for the first drill I had in mind. A few minutes later the other players started showing up. Emma and Zoe walked over to me and Jessi as we finished setting up. The two of them were good friends but they were also pretty opposite. Emma was tall and tan and athletic, and she could be a total klutz on the field unless she was in goal. Zoe was petite with short strawberry-blond hair, and she was super-agile and sure on her feet. She'd been playing forward a lot recently because she had this way of zigzagging through the other team's defenders and getting right to the goal.

"Yay! It's Devin's practice day!" Emma cheered.

"I found some new drills we can try," I said.

"Devin says we can make the play-offs if we keep winning games," Jessi reported.

Zoe cocked her head. "Us? Really?"

I laughed. "Why does everyone keep saying that? It's not impossible."

Jessi patted me on the back. "Well, we can dream."

"To dream the impossible dream!"

We all turned at the sound of someone singing in an operatic voice. It was Frida, of course. Besides playing soccer, she was a total drama nut.

"Bravo! Bravo!" Emma cried, clapping.

"Actually, it's *'brava'* when it's a girl," Frida corrected. "But thank you." She took a little bow.

Coach Flores blew the whistle, which meant it was time for practice to start. We ran to join the rest of the Kicks, and I was surprised to notice that it seemed not all the girls were there. I did a quick count—there were twelve of us, but there should have been nineteen.

"Where is everybody?" I asked.

Coach shrugged. "They must be running late. But go ahead and start, Devin."

I nodded. "Okay. Let's do some stretches to warm up."

I led everyone in stretches, and then we ran around the field once to get our hearts pumping. As I ran, I made a mental list of everyone who was missing—three seventh graders and four eighth graders, including Grace. It was kind of weird.

The missing players still hadn't showed up when we were done running, so I went ahead and started the first drill.

"Okay!" I told everyone. "So this first drill is a variation on Monkey in the Middle. There are a few ways to do it, but we're going to focus on our intercepting skills."

I counted down the line of players, "One, two, one, two," until everyone had a number. "Okay, ones, please form a circle inside that square we've marked out with cones. Twos, form a circle inside the other square."

My teammates formed the circles quickly, and then I pulled out two girls from each circle to stand in the middle—Brianna and Taylor in one circle, and Frida and Jade in the other.

"Okay. Here's how this works," I said. "Girls on the outside, you're playing offense. Your goal is to keep passing the ball to one another for as long as you can. Girls on the inside, you're defense. Your goal is to intercept or block the passes between the offensive players. If you succeed, the offensive player who made the pass has to switch places with you."

I threw a ball to each circle. "Ready, go!"

Emma made the first kick in her circle, and it flew right over Brianna's head.

"Whoops!" Emma cried.

"Got it!" Maya, an eighth grader who usually played midfielder, stopped the ball with her knee and sent it skidding across the circle, low but fast. This time Brianna stopped the ball with her foot. Then she and Maya switched places.

Both circles got the hang of it really quickly, and Coach Flores helped me out by giving pointers to the girls trying to defend. After a few minutes you could start to see what everyone's strengths and weaknesses were. Jade, an eighth grade defender, easily intercepted the first pass that came at her. Zoe, who was a strong offensive player when she was dribbling, was having trouble passing to players across the circle. She just didn't have enough power behind her kicks. And Frida was stuck in the middle for a long time. She couldn't get where she needed to be in time. But I knew that everyone was trying their hardest.

"Great job!" I called after we had played for about twenty minutes. "Let's clear the cones."

"Hey, there's Grace!" Brianna called out.

I turned and saw Grace and the rest of the missing girls walking onto the field. They looked puzzled to see us practicing.

I jogged up to Grace.

"Did you guys start already?" she asked.

I nodded. "Yeah, about a half hour ago."

She frowned. "But Coach Flores e-mailed that practice was starting late today."

Coach Flores had overheard. "I didn't do that. Are you sure it was from me?"

Grace and the other girls nodded.

"It came from your e-mail address," said Sarah.

Coach shook her head. "That is so strange. Maybe it was an old e-mail that you saw? That happens sometimes. An old e-mail pops up out of nowhere."

"Like it was stuck in limbo or something," Emma added.

"Well, sorry you guys missed the first drill, but we're about to do another one," I said. "Do you want to warm up first?"

"Just give us a minute to stretch," Grace replied.

I was feeling a little impatient, but I didn't show it. "We might as well all stretch!"

After a few more minutes of stretching, I clapped my hands, eager to start the next drill.

"It's time for a shoot-out! Emma, take the goal!"

Emma was kind of all over the place when she was on the field, but I'd discovered that she made an excellent goalie. She jogged over to the goal, and I got the other players to line up in two lines, with the first person in line facing the goal—one line on the right, and one line on the left.

"This one is fast and furious," I said. "Emma will start out as goalie. First player on the right will take a shot at the goal and then run to the back of the line. Then a player on the left will take a shot. Keep going until everyone has a turn, and then we'll switch goalies."

Giselle, an eighth grader with curly blond hair, looked at me with wide eyes. "You mean we *all* have to take the goal?"

"On a well-rounded team, everybody needs to know how to play every position," I told her. I knew that sounded kind of preachy, but I had done a lot of reading about coaching over the past few days to prep for this, and that idea had come up a lot. Giselle didn't look too happy, but I wasn't going to change the practice. We had to make sure we had a good backup goalie in case Emma couldn't play in a game.

"Ready, go!" I yelled once we were set up. Jessi ran up to make the first kick.

Wham! She sent the ball flying high and fast, and Emma had to jump up to block it. She slammed it down just as the next ball came whizzing past her feet.

Emma proved what a great goalie she was, because the pace was intense and she blocked more balls than she let get past her. When we came to the end of the line, I sent Jessi into the goal. She got into it with more energy than I had ever seen, diving and jumping.

Just like with the first drill, it became pretty clear what the players' strengths were, and who had goal-keeping in their blood. Sarah, a seventh grader, was really fast and kept her eye on the ball. And Zarine, who was in eighth grade and usually played midfield, made this amazing save where she jumped sideways to catch the ball in midair and then landed by somersaulting on the grass.

"Your turn, Devin!" Jessi called out when the last girl had taken her turn.

"Oh, yeah. Of course!" I replied, running to take my place. Just because I was running the practice didn't mean I couldn't participate in the drill.

I slipped on the goalie gloves and got ready for the onslaught. I didn't have to wait long.

Wham! Brianna sent a ball sailing past my head.

"I wasn't ready!" I protested.

"A goalie always needs to be ready!" Emma yelled back, laughing, and I knew she was right. I narrowed my eyes and waited for the next ball. Grace kicked it, and it came speeding across the grass, low and fast, aimed for the lower right corner of the goal. I dove for it, skidded across the grass, and blocked it just in time.

No sooner was I back on my feet than Sarah launched the next ball into the air, and I raced across the goal to stop it.

Wow, this is a pretty tough drill, I realized, but I didn't let on. I gave every shot my best, and managed to block about half of them. After the last shot blew past me, I jogged up to Emma.

"Have I told you lately what an awesome goalie you are?" I asked, breathing hard. "That is hard work."

Emma grinned. "Yeah, but I love it," she said. "Although, some nights I dream that soccer balls are flying past my head—like, thousands of them—and I can't stop them."

I nodded. "I can see why," I said, and then I turned to the rest of the team. "Okay, let's scrimmage! I'll count off teams."

We had all nineteen girls now, including me, so I put nine people on a team and I coached from the sideline. Since Zarine had done so well in the last drill, I put her in goal for her team. She seemed a little nervous at first, but I could see her get more comfortable with it as the scrimmage went on.

It seemed like only a few minutes had passed when Coach Flores tapped me on the shoulder.

"Devin, we should end the game," she said. "Great practice."

"Already?" I asked. "I was hoping to do one more quick drill at the end."

Coach nodded toward the parking lot, where some parents were already waiting in cars. "We're running a little late already. Sorry."

"More drills? You really are a *drill* sergeant," Jessi teased. "I, for one, am ready for a shower and some dinner."

"Admit it. It was fun," I said.

Frida walked up to us, her hands on her hips. "Fun and exhausting," she said.

After we put the equipment away, Jessi, Emma, Zoe, Frida, and I walked toward the parking lot.

"Hey, I wanted to tell you guys," Frida said. "So, you know how my mom made me play soccer? Well, she's so happy that I am putting my 'best effort' into it, as she says, that she signed me up for a weekly acting class. Isn't that great? I start tomorrow."

"That sounds perfect for you," Emma agreed.

"It's a win-win," Frida said. "I ended up liking soccer, and now I get to keep acting, too."

I wasn't so sure. "You start tomorrow? Couldn't it wait until after soccer season? What if it interferes with your practice?"

"Relax, Devin," Frida said. "It's only one day a week, when we don't have practice."

"In Devin's perfect world every day would be a practice day," Jessi teased. "Practice after breakfast, practice during lunch break . . ."

"Midnight practice," Emma joined in. "And sunrise practice."

"Okay, okay, I get it," I said, laughing. "I'm happy for you, Frida. Seriously."

"Be happy for me once my mom lets me start auditioning again," Frida said. "Shawna Young from my old acting class just got a part on a TV show, and I *know* I'm a better actor than she is."

Just then my mom's car pulled up, so I waved to my friends. "Got to go. See you tomorrow."

I ran to the car, and when I opened the door, really loud pop music blared out. In the backseat my sister Maisie was bopping up and down.

"Seriously, does it have to be this loud?" I asked.

"Yes, it does!" Maisie yelled from the back.

Mom turned the sound down a little bit. "How did practice go?" she asked.

"Great," I replied. "I didn't get to do all the drills I wanted, but the ones we did were really good."

"Of course they were," Mom said. "That's my dedicated Devin."

"Turn it up!" Maisie yelled.

Everyone said that Maisie and I looked alike, and I guessed we did, because we both had brown eyes and straight brown hair, although Maisie's was shorter than mine. But just because we looked alike didn't mean we *were* alike. I was a pretty chill person (well, except on the soccer field), and Maisie was like an eight-year-old tornado.

"Maisie, please use your car voice," Mom scolded, and I quickly dug my earbuds out of my duffel bag and turned on my own music so I could make it home without going crazy.

Once we got home, I quickly showered and then turned on my laptop in my bedroom. After Kara's last visit we'd decided to do a webcam chat once a day if we could, so we could see each other's faces. But sometimes it was hard to find the right time because it was always three hours later in Connecticut.

"Devin!" Kara cried happily when her face popped up on my screen. The webcam was amazing because I could see every freckle on Kara's face.

"Hey!" I said. "What's up?"

"Still dreaming about my weekend in California with you," she answered. "It's amazing there! It's so sunny and beautiful. And I still can't believe that we actually went to Hollywood. And how close you are to Disneyland! It must be like being on vacation all the time."

"It kind of felt like that at first," I admitted. "But now it's like, you know, life. Like, tonight I have a ton of homework."

"I did too," Kara said, making a face. "But I just finished. High-five!"

She held her palm up in front of the camera, and I did the same. Kara cracked me up sometimes.

"Oh, hey," I said. "I have been dying to tell you something all day. I just figured out that the Kicks might have a chance at the play-offs—if we focus. Can you believe that? After those losses we had in the beginning."

"That's awesome," Kara said. "Focusing is good. Although, I don't know how you can focus with that guy Steven staring at you the whole time."

I blushed. "What?" I asked, but I knew what she meant.

"Steven, that guy with the spiky hair," Kara replied. "When I saw you in that game against the Panthers, he sat near us, and I swear he was staring at you the whole entire game."

"He was not," I protested.

"He's cute!" Kara said. "I wish somebody that cute would stare at me."

"Fine, he's cute," I admitted. "But I can't think about stuff like that right now. I need to focus on school and on the Kicks until the season is over."

"Maybe Steven is thinking about you right now," Kara teased. "Devin and Steven. It kind of rhymes."

Then she began to sing, "Devin and Steven. Devin and Steven—"

"No distractions!" I yelled, and then we both collapsed into giggles.

Every time I talked to Kara, I realized how much I missed her. The webcam was nice, but it was just not the same as being with her in person. Sometimes I daydreamed that Kara and her family moved out to California and she joined the Kicks. If that could have happened, I thought my life would have been pretty perfect!

CHAPTER TWO

"Devin!" Frida cried as I walked into the locker room on Wednesday after school. We had a rare afternoon game against the Victorton Eagles. We had lost to the Eagles once before and I really wanted to beat them this time.

Frida was sitting on a bench in front of a row of lockers. "I need inspiration," she pleaded.

"Oh! I got one!" Emma called as she stuck her head around the row of lockers. "Frida, you can be an alien who is sent undercover to Earth to learn about what life is like for a typical middle school girl. So you join the soccer team and stuff."

"Hmmmm." Frida considered this. "Am I an evil alien? Like, am I going to use the things I learn to take over the world?"

"Nah." Emma shook her head. "You're peaceful. You're trying to figure out if humans are ready to know about alien life or if they'll just freak out. And if you find us worthy, you can share all your awesome alien technology with us."

"I like that," Frida said. She closed her eyes tightly. "Okay, need to find my motivation."

Some people might have thought that Frida was weird. But we'd figured out that if she had a role to play during a soccer game, she'd play a lot better. Whatever worked, right? I left her to it and walked to the next row of lockers, where Emma, Jessi, and Zoe were getting changed.

"Victorton Eagles are going down!" Jessi said with a grin. "I feel like the Kicks are unstoppable!"

"I can't believe how good we're doing, especially after how rough the start of the season was, especially for me," Zoe said, and she shook her head.

"I knew you could do it, Zoe!" Emma cheered. I swore Emma had an endless supply of enthusiasm.

"Yeah, you've totally conquered your soccer stage fright," Jessi said.

Zoe smiled shyly. "Frida's tricks really work. During the last game I just imagined that everyone in the stands was my mom, and I calmed right down."

"Can you imagine if everyone in the stands were Maisie?" I joked. "Wait, that might not be so bad. She could annoy the other team into distraction."

My friends laughed as I sat down on the bench and started pulling my cleats out of my duffel bag. Then a garbled voice sounded over the loudspeaker. "Devin Burke, please report to the main office."

"Ooooohhhh!" my teammates cried as if I were in trouble.

"But we've got a game!" I complained as Coach Flores walked into the locker room.

"Better hustle, then, Devin," Coach said.

I sighed. I had wasted time talking when I should have been getting my uniform on. And the main office was on the other side of the school! I wondered what they wanted me for. I was sure I wasn't in trouble for anything. At least, I was pretty sure.

"Okay," I said to Coach. "I'll be back soon!"

I sprinted out of the locker room, nearly colliding with Giselle and Grace, and then took off running as fast as I could. Oh, well. I could consider it my warm-up for the game.

I skidded to a halt in the main office, panting.

"My name is Devin Burke," I said in between breaths. "I was paged over the loudspeaker to come to the office."

"Ah, Devin." Mrs. Wolbach, one of the secretaries, smiled at me. "Your mom is on the phone."

She pointed to a phone on a table in the corner of the office. The receiver was off the hook and sitting on the table.

Why wouldn't my mom call me on my cell phone? I wondered. That was what she usually did. And she knew I had a game after school today too. I started to get nervous, wondering if everything was okay.

I picked up the receiver. "Hello?"

A dial tone hummed on the other end, so I told Mrs. Wolbach.

"Go ahead and call her back," she said. "Maybe the call got disconnected."

I quickly punched in my mom's cell phone number.

"Devin?" My mom sounded surprised when she heard my voice. "Don't you have a game? Maisie and I are sitting in the bleachers now."

"Yes, but you called me," I said. "I mean, the secretary, Mrs. Wolbach, said that you called the main office asking for me. They paged me from the locker room to come and take the call."

"I'm sorry, honey, but I didn't call. Maybe they got your name mixed up with someone else?" Mom suggested.

"Maybe, but I gotta go!" I cried. "I'm not even in my uniform yet!"

"Good luck!" Mom said before hanging up.

I quickly told Mrs. Wolbach what my mom had said.

"I could have sworn the woman said she wanted to talk to her daughter, Devin Burke," Mrs. Wolbach said, and frowned. "That's odd. There *is* a boy named Devon Ernst in the sixth grade. I suppose I could have mixed you two up."

"Okay, but I have to run!" I said. I didn't want to miss the game!

"Go, and have a great game!" Mrs. Wolbach gave me a smile, and I darted out of the office, running as fast as I could.

I cut outside and ran past the field because I figured it

was shorter, plus I didn't want to get in trouble for running in the halls. The Kangaroos were already on the field, warming up. I had to hustle!

"Hurry, Devin!" Jessi yelled. "We need you out here for the sock swap!"

"I'm coming!" I yelled back as I careened into the locker room. I ran to the bench and went to grab my duffel bag.

Only problem: There was no duffel bag! My cleats were sitting on the bench, right where I had left them, but my duffel bag was missing. In it was the rest of my uniform and gear, and the makings for my lucky pink headband.

Had I put my duffel bag on another bench? I raced up and down the locker room, checking each row. Then I really started to panic and began to open and close all the lockers, slamming the doors shut when I couldn't find my bag.

Frantic, I ran outside and found Coach Flores.

"Devin! What's going on?" she asked. "Why aren't you dressed?"

"Coach! I can't find my duffel bag," I said. "I left it on the bench when I got called to the office, and it was gone when I got back. It's got everything in it!"

"It's got to be there somewhere," Coach said.

I shook my head. "I looked everywhere. I swear."

"Uh-oh." Coach frowned. "You can't play without your team uniform, or without your shin guards."

"I know!" I wailed. No way did I want to miss a game!

Coach's face brightened, and she snapped her fingers. "I have an idea! I've got a spare uniform, shin guards, and some duct tape. Follow me."

We ran to her office, and she handed me a blue-and-white Kangaroo uniform, some shin guards, and a roll of black duct tape.

"Quick! Get changed, and when you're done, meet me on the sidelines. I'll use the duct tape to put your number on the back."

I changed in record time. My hands wandered to my head, looking for my pink headband. That was a pregame ritual I had brought with me from Connecticut. Kara and I always wore pink headbands at every game. Not only did they help us stand out, but we were convinced they brought us luck, too. I let out a big sigh.

"This is the first time I'll ever play without my pink headband," I said to Coach when I got outside.

"At least you'll be able to play," Coach said. "Now turn around."

She quickly spelled out my usually lucky thirteen onto the back of my shirt with duct tape.

"All right. You're good," she told me. "Don't worry. We'll find your bag after the game. Now let's hurry!"

The game was about to begin, and I looked around at the Kicks' legs. Everyone was wearing mismatched socks, and I could see I'd missed another pregame ritual, the sock swap. It was something Jessi and I had done together at the tryouts for the Kangaroos. Before long the entire team had joined in. Before every game we got together in a circle and handed one of our socks to the person on our left. Jessi had even come up with a silly way of putting the socks on—for luck, she said. It had worked, because as soon as the entire team had started doing the sock swap together, we'd started improving.

No pink headband. No sock swap. I hoped this wasn't a bad omen. The confidence I had felt earlier that afternoon began to disappear, and was replaced by a group of hyperactive butterflies flying around in my stomach. Not a good way to start a game!

"What happened?" Jessi asked, eyeing me curiously as we took to the field. "Are you in trouble? And what's with the uniform?"

"Long story, but I'm not in trouble," I said. "But my duffel bag—with my uniform, gear, and pink wrap for my headband—are missing. Did you see it?"

Jessi shook her head. "It was there when we left the locker room. I remember that. Right next to your cleats."

I was totally confused. What had happened to my bag? It hadn't just gotten up and walked out of the locker room. But before I could try to forget about that and turn my attention to the Victorton Eagles, Jessi dropped a bombshell.

"Don't freak out," she warned me. Why do people tell you that? As soon as you hear the words "freak out," that's what you do—freak! "But Mirabelle is up in the stands."

She pointed to a dark-haired girl.

"Oh, great," I groaned. "Why would she even show up here? She hated being on this team."

"No idea," Jessi said. "But if she calls us losers one more time, she'll have to deal with me."

Emma walked up behind us. "Mirabelle did us a favor when she transferred to Pinewood. Her negative energy was totally bad for the team. The Kicks are better off without her."

Mirabelle's perfect white teeth glistened in the sun as she laughed at something the girl next to her said. Ugh. Had Mirabelle come to intimidate us from the stands?

"And that," Jessi continued, pointing to the blond girl sitting next to Mirabelle, "is Jamie Quinn, captain of the Riverdale Rams. She and Mirabelle are friends. They met on their travel team."

Jessi always had a lot of insider info on Mirabelle. That was because not only were they neighbors, but they used to be besties once upon a time. But both Jessi and Mirabelle had changed a lot. They were no longer friends, and often they were openly hostile toward each other. Actually, Mirabelle was openly hostile to a lot of people, not just Jessi.

"They must be here to scope out the competition," Jessi said, and grinned. "Let's make 'em worried!"

Easy for Jessi to say, I thought as I suppressed a groan. She hadn't lost her bag and hadn't had to make a mad dash across the entire school. This game was already not turning out how I had hoped!

The whistle blew and the game started. I felt a little distracted and had a hard time getting my head in the game at first.

"Offsides!" The ref blew his whistle at me after I zoomed past an Eagles defender, trying to connect with a pass Grace had sent my way.

Ouch. "Sorry, guys," I said to my teammates.

"No problem, Devin," Grace answered.

"Kick that ball and make a score. Come on, Kicks, we want to see more!" Emma cheered from the goal as an Eagles striker swooped in with a scoring chance. Emma dove on the ball and stopped it in its tracks.

"Yes!" I called, pumping my fist in the air. Emma grinned and clapped her goalie gloves together.

Once the ball was back in play, I managed to steal a pass. Charging up the field, I heard my teammates shouting "Go, go, go!" Out of the corner of my eye, I saw an Eagles defender swooping down on me. I turned to get a better look at her, but my hair fell over my eyes, blocking my vision.

Rats! I had been wearing my pink headband for luck for so long that I'd forgot it served a functional purpose too, not just a superstitious one!

The defender took advantage of my momentary blindness and stole the ball from me, spiking it to an Eagles midfielder, who lofted it with ease to a striker. But what the Eagles striker didn't know was that Frida the alien was playing defense for the Kicks today!

"Sorry, earthling, but you must be immobilized," she said in a strange, almost robotic voice. The Eagles player, a tall, thin girl with her dark black hair pulled into a high ponytail, got a nervous look on her face. Her eyes grew wide, and she fumbled slightly, losing control of the ball, and Frida quickly took advantage of the situation.

The striker turned to another Eagles player as Frida punted the ball safely away from our goal. "What was that?"

"Don't worry. That's Frida. She's an alien from another planet," Emma called from the goal. "But she's totally harmless. She won't hurt you."

The Eagles players exchanged anxious glances while the Kicks cracked up. Even though I was feeling flustered from the uniform fiasco, Mirabelle turning up, and my missing headband costing me a goal, I had to laugh at Frida's antics. The Eagles players had no idea how to deal with an alien on the soccer field!

The action continued, fast and furious. Alandra passed the ball to Grace, who was within striking distance of the Eagles goal. The pass went high, and Grace dove into the ball, slamming it with her head into the goal before landing on her arms in the grass.

The crowd cheered. "Awesome diving header!" Giselle yelled.

"Wow!" I said. "I didn't know you could do that."

Grace laughed and shook her head. "I didn't know I could do that either. I'm so glad I pulled it off."

Zoe managed to score three goals practically in a row, which caused more excitement.

"Zoe, the scoring machine!" Jessi yelled.

"Way to go, Zoe!" Sarah called, and Zoe gave a shy smile.

At halftime we were up 4–2. I still felt like I didn't have my act together, so Brianna subbed in for me as a striker. Luckily, my teammates had brought their A games with them, and I watched the action, proud of my team. I was impressed with the way Jessi and Grace worked together, using short passes to move the ball down the field. The Eagles' defense was lacking in organization, so Zoe and Brianna were on the lookout for an open passing lane. Jessi and Grace moved the ball back and forth, waiting for the perfect opportunity. Finally they spotted it: a break in between two of the Eagles defenders. Jessi had possession of the ball and lofted a kick through the space. Both Zoe and Brianna were waiting for that very moment, and they both carelessly raced to get the ball, forgetting about each other in their eagerness.

Boom! They collided, hard. Zoe tumbled to the ground, putting her hand out to brace her fall. Brianna got control of the ball and punched it past the Eagles goalie. Goal! The final whistle sounded. We had won!

I rushed onto the field along with the other Kicks who'd been on the sideline. Everyone began hugging one another and cheering with happiness.

"We are the Kicks. We can't be beat, because we got the power to knock you off your feet," Emma cheered.

"Oh, no!" Jessi groaned as she rushed over to Zoe. "Someone got knocked off their feet, and it wasn't an Eagle."

We all watched Jessi race over to Zoe, who was still sprawled in the grass after her collision with Brianna. Coach Flores stood anxiously over her. Tears streamed down Zoe's face as she cradled her right arm with her left hand. I ran over there as fast as I could.

"Zoe, are you all right?" I asked.

CHAPTER THREE

Zoe looked pale. "My wrist really hurts," she said softly.

Just then Zoe's whole family descended onto the field—her mom, dad, and her three older sisters, who were all petite with strawberry-blond hair, just like Zoe.

Coach Flores turned to us. "Great game, girls. Why don't you all go change while Zoe's parents and I evaluate her injury. I'm sure she's going to be just fine."

"Bye, Zoe." Emma kneeled down and kissed her on the cheek. "Feel better!"

The team drifted off the field, calling out get-well wishes to Zoe as we left.

"Poor Zoe!" Jessi said once we were back in the locker room.

"It should have been me instead!" Frida wailed dramatically, throwing a hand onto her forehead.

"No, it was my fault," Brianna said. She looked upset. "I wasn't paying attention. Once I saw that you guys got the ball through, that's all I focused on. I didn't realize Zoe was going for it too."

Anna, a seventh grader who was friends with both Brianna and Sarah, put an arm around Brianna's shoulder. "It was an accident," she reminded her. "Accidents happen in soccer sometimes."

"And on the bright side, we did win," Emma said.

"Maybe, but I'm so worried about Zoe," Frida said.

Jessi's eyes narrowed. "It's that Mirabelle. She probably put a hex on Zoe or something."

"Mirabelle?" Anna asked, her big brown eyes getting even bigger in surprise. "What does Mirabelle have to do with it?"

At the mention of Mirabelle's name, a crowd gathered, curious to hear what we were talking about. A lot of people were still mad at her. When she was on the Kangaroos, she called her fellow teammates losers all the time, which was not the best way to make friends.

Jessi filled everyone in. "So Mirabelle was in the stands watching the game, along with Jamie, the captain of the Rams. I bet they put the evil eye on us!"

"Most likely they were here to size us up," Brianna said thoughtfully. "After all, we did go from being the worst team in the league to being serious competition."

Emma shrugged. "Who cares? We need to hurry up and get changed so we can see how Zoe is doing!"

In all the excitement I had almost forgotten about my missing bag! I had nothing to hold my cleats and my borrowed uniform.

"Hey, everyone!" I called loudly over the din of lockers being opened and the girls chatting about the Mirabelle news. "My soccer bag is missing. It's hot pink and black." A lot of the girls had black-and-white or black-and-pink bags. "It also has a soccer key chain attached to it, with little US flags on it."

My dad had gotten me that key chain during the summer Olympics, when my entire family had watched the US women's soccer team win the gold! I'd spent a lot of time that summer daydreaming about being on the Olympic team myself one day.

"Sorry, Devin, haven't seen it!"

"Nope, not here!"

"We'll keep a lookout for it!"

The Kicks' voices echoed through the locker room, the same response over and over. My shoulders slumped in disappointment.

I folded the spare uniform and tucked it under my arm, my cleats dangling from my hand. Emma and Jessi were changed and ready to go, and I noticed that Jessi had a really serious look on her face.

"Worried about Zoe?" I asked.

"Yes, but it's not just that," she replied. "Something weird is going on. Strange e-mails. A missing bag. And now Zoe's hurt."

"Are you saying they're all related or something?" Emma asked.

"I'm not sure," Jessi said. She tapped Sarah on the shoulder as she walked past.

"Can I see your phone?"

Sarah stopped. "Sure," she replied.

"I need to see that e-mail you got from Coach Flores on Monday," Jessi said.

Sarah nodded and scrolled through her screen. "Here it is."

Jessi looked at it. "Aha! See? This e-mail is from coachflores@mailmee.us, but Coach's address is coachflores@smartphone.net!"

"Are you sure?" I asked.

Jessi held out her own phone. "See? It's right here."

I looked at Jessi's phone, and she was right. "Well, maybe that's an old e-mail address of hers."

Jessi's face fell. "Yeah, you might be right."

"Can we talk about this later?" Emma interrupted, her voice anxious. "I want to find out if Zoe's okay."

"Yeah, of course," I said.

We left the locker room, and my mom and Maisie were waiting for us. My dad was at work, so he had given my mom the video camera to record the game. Dad came to every game he could and recorded it. He was my biggest fan! But Maisie was holding the video camera now.

"I don't know how to work that thing," my mom

complained as she gave me a hug and a kiss. "So Maisie was today's videographer."

I rolled my eyes. Whenever Maisie got her hands on any kind of recording device, she used it to make what she called the Maisie Show. Basically it was Maisie singing and telling corny jokes and long, rambling stories. I'd put it like this: It was not likely to be picked up for television anytime soon.

Maisie gave me a smirk, which made me wonder how much of our game was actually on there!

"Mom, how is Zoe?" I asked. Jessi and Emma gathered around, concerned.

"It looks like she put her hand down to break her fall when she fell, and when she did that, she hurt her wrist," Mom explained. "Her parents took her to the hospital for X-rays. They want to make sure nothing is broken."

"Can we go see her?"

My mom nodded. "I knew you'd want to, Devin. Jessi and Emma, if you would like to ride with us, I already talked to your moms about it."

"Of course!" Emma said.

Jessi nodded in agreement. "We Kicks have to stick together!"

We piled into the van, and as soon as we strapped on our seat belts, my mom handed out water bottles to everyone. "You girls need to hydrate!" she said. "That was quite a game."

I exchanged smiles with my friends. My mom was a

health nut, and her biggest worry in the world was that I would dehydrate, wither up, and blow away on the next strong breeze.

At the hospital there was no sign of Zoe, but her oldest sister, Jayne, sat in the waiting room. My mom went over and started talking to her. Jayne was a senior in high school and very mature. Like Zoe and her two other sisters, Jayne was a fashionista and looked like she'd just stepped out of a magazine. Zoe said it helped to have three older sisters' closets she could raid!

"Zoe's getting her X-rays now," my mom said after Jayne was done filling her in. "Her parents are with her. So let's just take a seat and wait."

Maisie sat in a chair with her handheld video game player to occupy her. I noticed Mom had also slipped her a snack bag of cookies, a rare treat that was also guaranteed to keep Maisie quiet and happy. Emma slumped into a seat, but Jessi and I paced back and forth nervously. Of course I was worried about Zoe, but to tell the truth I was also worried about what Zoe's injury would mean to the team.

Since we had won today's game, we had a chance at the play-offs. Most likely we'd need to win at least three more games, but there were other teams competing for the third and fourth spots too, mainly the Rams and the Tigers. I walked back and forth, running numbers and scenarios through my mind.

"Earth to Devin!" Jessi called out, a grin on her face.

"Zoe's not dying or anything. Don't look so worried!"

"It's not that." I shook my head. "I'm trying to figure out exactly how many wins we'll need to make play-offs, but it's complicated. The Eagles need to lose two more games, and we need to have three more wins, I think. But I'm not sure. It's kind of confusing."

Jessi frowned. "Devin, Zoe is hurt, and all you can think about are stats?"

Jessi putting it like that made me feel kind of heartless. I immediately stopped in my tracks as a horrified look crossed my face. "Oh, no. I didn't mean it like that! Of course I'm worried about Zoe."

Emma turned to me. "I get it, Devin. We need a captain who wants to win!"

"Thanks," I said. "And it's not just about winning. I mean, I've wanted to be a professional soccer player since I was eight years old. And colleges look at championship teams when they recruit."

"College recruiters look at *middle school* championship teams?" Jessi said.

I shrugged. "Maybe not," I said. "But it can't hurt to win either."

Just then Zoe and her parents walked into the waiting room. Zoe's right wrist was wrapped in a bandage and her arm was in a sling. Her face was still pale and she looked tired, but she brightened up when she saw us waiting for her.

"Zoe!" Emma launched off the chair and ran over to her.

Zoe backed up and put her good hand out. "Whoa! I don't want to get knocked over again," she said with a laugh.

"It's not broken, but it's a severe sprain," Mrs. Quinlan was telling my mom.

"So can you play?" The words popped right out of my mouth before I could stop them. Jessi shot me a stern look. "I mean, you don't really need your hands in soccer, unless you're a goalie. And I'm so glad it's not broken!"

Zoe sighed. "The doctor says it could take three or four weeks to heal," she said. "I asked him if I could play soccer, but he said that wouldn't be a good idea, because if I fall on it again, it could get hurt worse."

"I agree," Zoe's mom said firmly. "And I know that the school has a strict policy about keeping players with injuries off the field. Remember when your sister hurt her knee?"

Zoe sighed. "I know."

"Does it hurt?" Emma asked, her eyes wide with concern.

"Not too bad anymore; they gave me some ibuprofen," Zoe said.

"We're just glad you're okay," Jessi said as she gingerly gave Zoe a hug, trying to steer clear of her right wrist.

I *was* glad Zoe was going to be okay. But I couldn't help wondering what it would mean for the Kicks.

Once we all knew that Zoe was all right, I had to tell my mom and dad about my missing uniform. Mom totally freaked out.

"You must have misplaced it," she kept saying. "Did you retrace your steps?"

"I looked everywhere!" I told her over and over, but she didn't seem to believe me. But she did take me to the mall at the last minute to get some new shin guards, and I was grateful for that. I was also glad that I'd had my cell phone tucked into my jeans pocket that day, not in my bag like I usually did. She would have gone seriously nuts if I had lost that, too. And luckily, I still had plenty of the pink sports wrap at home that I used to make my headbands.

One thing was still worrying me when I got to the practice field the next day. With Zoe out we were going to need to come up with some new formations for the field, and quick. Because play-offs were looming, I began to get nervous. Our team had just started to turn things around. Could we bounce back from a blow like this? Coach Flores was running today's practice, but I knew she was always open to ideas.

I pulled Grace aside before we started our scrimmage to share with her what I was thinking.

"I think we need to come up with some serious changes to compensate for Zoe's absence," I told her.

Grace frowned. "Zoe's really awesome and all, but we're a team. I think we've got some good players we can sub in for her as striker."

"But in that Pinewood game we totally relied on Zoe to take the Panthers by surprise," I said, making my case. "And Zoe really carried the offense for us against Victorton, too. It's going to throw everyone off to not have her out there."

Grace looked at me for a second without saying anything. She was usually pretty quiet but always very focused, and she was a natural athlete.

"You have a point, Devin," she said slowly. "If there's something you want to try, we should do it now at practice."

I grinned. "Thanks," I said. "Let's tell Coach."

Grace and I approached Coach Flores. "So, I was thinking we should try something new for the scrimmage today," I said. "How about using a two-four-two offensive formation?"

Coach raised an eyebrow. "Are you sure that's the right formation for our team?"

I had been researching different formations ever since Zoe had become injured. When we scrimmage, we divide the team into two teams of nine. We usually have three on defense, three midfielders, and two strikers on each side: three-three-two. In a two-four-two formation, we'd have a stronger midfield. Maybe that would compensate for losing Zoe, whose speed often confused the opposing defenders.

"Can we at least try it?" I asked. "I think it might give us an advantage."

Coach shrugged. "Why not? Let's give it a try."

She divided the team into two groups for the scrimmage, and I assigned positions.

"Frida, you move to midfield!" I called as we jogged onto the field. "Jessi, try out defense."

"What?" Jessi asked, puzzled. "I thought I could sub in for Zoe."

"We're trying out something new, and I need you as a sweeper," I told her.

I gave a quick explanation of the formation to the girls, but I could tell they were a little confused. We began the scrimmage anyway, and chaos soon erupted.

On defense Sarah got dragged infield, so when Jessi and Giselle tried to compensate, it left massive holes in our defense.

Megan took advantage and scored on Emma.

"Where am I supposed to be?" Anna called, confused. As a midfielder she had to cover different areas of the field while constantly switching from blocking attackers to trying to pass the ball to the forwards. Frida also looked lost. Soon other voices could be heard, shouting in confusion.

"Hey, you're supposed to be here!"

"Should I be helping defense or offense right now?"

Coach blew her whistle. "Stop! Okay, it was worth a shot, Devin, but I think we'll put this formation on the back burner for a while."

"But, Coach," I pleaded, my words coming out in a rush. "Maybe if we move Jessi to midfield and—"

"Devin, relax." Coach placed a hand on my shoulder and smiled at me. "This isn't working. Let's try something else. We can still have a good practice today, don't worry."

She began talking to the team, organizing us for a quick, basic scrimmage.

I let out a deep sigh. Of course Coach wouldn't be worried. She didn't realize yet that we'd never make the play-offs without Zoe. And today's practice was proof!

CHAPTER FOUR

After practice Frida's mom dropped Jessi, Emma, Frida, and me off at the frozen yogurt place in town. We went right from the field, still in our grass-stained uniforms, but I didn't care. I felt like I had eaten lunch an eternity ago, the sun was hot, and a cup of frozen yogurt was going to hit the spot like nothing else. We found a table by the window, and soon I was settled in my seat, eating a cup of vanilla with fresh strawberry and kiwi on top.

"This definitely makes up for that lousy practice," I said after my first spoonful, and Jessi and Emma looked at each other.

"What?" I asked, putting down my spoon.

"That practice was doomed from the start," Jessi said with her usual bluntness. "What was up with switching around everybody's positions?"

"What is up is that I'm trying to figure out how we're

going to win without Zoe," I replied. "We've all got to be willing to try new things."

"Well, maybe switching positions isn't the best answer," Emma said diplomatically. "Maybe Coach has some ideas."

"I love Coach Flores, but you know how laid-back she can be," I countered. "Anyway, it was worth a try, right?"

"Just please don't make me play midfielder again," Frida said. "I feel much safer back by the goal."

"Safer? With all those strikers coming at you?" I asked.

Frida shrugged. "I don't know. I guess I found my comfort zone."

My feelings were starting to get a tiny bit hurt, so I was glad when Jessi changed the subject.

"So, Devin, you never found your duffel bag?" she asked.

I shook my head. "It's so weird. It's like it just disappeared. Mom even called the school janitor and asked him to keep an eye out for it around the school, but he hasn't seen it."

Frida's dark eyes got wide. "It must have been foul play," she said, lowering her voice dramatically.

"You mean like a chicken took it?" Emma asked, giggling.

"Not *fowl* play. *Foul* play," Frida said. "I think your duffel bag was stolen."

"That's exactly what I've been thinking!" Jessi agreed.

"But who would want to steal a uniform and some shin guards?" I asked. "I could see that if I'd left it on the field or something, but this was in the locker room. Somebody would have had to go to a lot of effort to get in there and take it."

"Unless it didn't take any effort at all," Frida said, pausing dramatically. (To be fair, she did *most* things dramatically.) "It must have been someone on the team!"

Emma gasped. "No way! Who would do that? And why?"

"Reveeeeenge," Frida said, stretching out the word. "Or power. We're going to be doing all these Shakespeare scenes in my acting class, and there's tons of stuff like that in his plays."

"That is ridiculous," I said. "First of all, who would want to get revenge on me? For what?"

"Then maybe it's a power grab," Frida suggested. "Like when Macbeth destroyed all of his enemies so he could become king."

Jessi raised an eyebrow. "So you're saying that somebody wants to take over as co-captain and so they stole Devin's uniform? That's kind of a stretch."

"Yeah, especially since nobody else really wanted the job," I reminded everyone.

"Maybe it's not so serious," Emma tossed out. "Maybe it's like a prank. My cousin plays high school football, and the senior boys always prank the younger boys."

Jessi nodded. "That's true. And what about that weird e-mail that went out to some of the girls? If Coach Flores didn't send it, that's kind of like a prank."

I thought about this. "So you think one of the eighth graders did it?" I asked. "But that doesn't make sense. Most of the girls who got the e-mail were eighth graders."

"Well, maybe it's not the eighth graders," Jessi said. "But it could still be somebody on the team."

"The Mystery Prankster!" Frida said in an ominous tone.

I frowned. "Stealing my duffel bag could have kept me out of the game. I don't think anyone on the team would pull a prank that would jeopardize a game, would they?"

Everyone was quiet for a little bit, and I knew they were silently agreeing with me. Finally Frida spoke up.

"Hmm. I still think treachery is afoot," she said.

"Okay, Shakespeare. Chill out," Jessi said, laughing.

Just then Emma's phone beeped.

"It's from Zoe," she reported, looking at the screen. "She says she misses us and she's going to come to practice tomorrow to watch, even though she can't play. Yay! You know, maybe we should do something fun with her after practice. I know it hasn't been easy for her, getting around school in her sling and all that."

"It hasn't," Frida said. "Brendan Insler has been following her around so he can carry her books. Zoe's totally annoyed."

"Brendan?" I asked. I still didn't know most of the kids in seventh grade.

"Actually, I think he's totally cute," Jessi said.

"You think every boy is totally cute," I pointed out, and Jessi gave me a light punch on the arm.

"Then we definitely need to cheer her up," Emma said. "We should go to the mall after practice since tomorrow's Friday."

"Only if we all shower and change first," Jessi argued, looking down at her dirty uniform. "I am not going to walk around the mall all muddy and nasty."

"I'll ask my mom if I can go," I said.

"Speaking of moms." Frida nodded toward the door, where her mom's car was waiting. "It's time to go!"

We cleaned up our table, went outside, and piled into Mrs. Rivera's car. She drove each one of us home, which was nice. When I got inside, Dad was making dinner. Even though I'd eaten a frozen yogurt, I was still hungry, and I eagerly approached the stove.

"What are we having?" I asked.

"It's Maisie's night to choose," Dad said. "So . . ."

"Noooo!" I wailed. "Not tuna casserole again!"

When I was little (and Maisie was just a baby) my mom got this idea that we could each pick out what we ate for dinner one night a week, so we wouldn't argue so much when she forced healthy food on us all the other days. It worked out for a long time, because Maisie mostly picked chicken fingers and mac and cheese when she was little. But three years ago she fell in love with our aunt Sally's tuna casserole, and now she had asked for it every week for three years.

"Maisie, how about tacos next week?" I asked when we sat down to eat. "You love tacos."

"I can get tacos at a restaurant," Maisie shot back. "But Dad is the only one who makes tuna casserole like Aunt Sally."

"How about . . . ravioli, then?" I asked. "You love ravioli, too."

"I also love tuna casserole," Maisie said stubbornly.

I sighed and picked through the mushy mess of noodles, tuna, sauce, cheese, and peas on my plate, pushing the peas to the side. I didn't mind snow peas in Chinese food or edamame when we went to the Japanese restaurant, but mushy peas . . . ugh.

"Hey, can I go to the mall tomorrow?" I asked as we finished up eating.

"With whom?" Mom asked. (She was the kind of mom who used proper grammar at all times.)

"Jessi, Emma, Zoe, and Frida," I said. "To cheer up Zoe."

"And who's driving?" Mom asked.

"I'm not sure," I replied.

Mom nodded. "I'll text the moms and we'll figure it out. But it's fine with me if it's fine with your dad."

"Sure, why not?" Dad said. "You've been practicing and studying a lot lately. It's nice that you're going out with your friends. Just not too late."

"Of course. We have practice Saturday morning," I replied.

Everyone's parents agreed, so we were all pretty excited at practice the next day. It was a good practice too, since we all played our usual positions during the scrimmage and nobody got confused. When it was over, we showered and got changed, and Zoe's mom drove us to the mall.

The Sun Center mall was basically like the malls back in Connecticut, except for the palm trees out front. There was a food court, and tons of stores. And lots of kids went there just to hang out and stuff. I was psyched because Mrs. Quinlan dropped us off at the entrance right by the Sports World store.

"Awesome," I said as we all walked inside. "I've been reading about these new limited-edition soccer cleats. They're supposed to be for traction and for speed. I'd love to try on a pair."

Jessi shook her head. "I swear if they opened up your skull, they'd find a soccer ball inside there instead of a brain."

"Actually, I wouldn't mind looking at the pro jerseys," Emma piped up. "They've got some cool new ones."

So we spent some time in Sports World, and then Jessi insisted that we check out her favorite clothing store, Shine. Jessi walked up to a display of scarves, picked up a shimmery gold one, and then draped it on Zoe's arm.

"Some bling for your sling," she joked, and we all cracked up. Frida and Jessi tried on some outfits, but I could tell it was bumming out Zoe a little bit because she couldn't easily try anything on.

"Maybe we should get going," I said to Jessi as I nodded toward the door. Jessi looked up, and her eyes narrowed angrily. Wow, I'd had no idea Jessi was such a serious shopper.

"Sorry," I started, wondering what was up, but then I followed Jessi's gaze and saw Mirabelle at the front of the store, browsing through a rack of earrings.

"Hey, Mirabelle," Jessi called out, and Mirabelle looked up, surprised to see her. Jessi gestured toward a mirror on the wall. "There's a mirror over here. You can take a look in it if you want to know what a real loser looks like. You may have noticed, but there are none on the Kicks anymore. Not since you left."

Whoa. That was pretty harsh, even though it was nothing compared to all the things Mirabelle had said and done to the Kicks when she'd been on our team. Emma and Zoe exchanged shocked glances. I was surprised to see a hurt look cross Mirabelle's face for a moment, but she quickly recovered and put on her usual smug smile.

"No, thanks," she said. She put her hands on her hips and glared at Jessi. "I'm a Pinewood Panther now, so I don't have to share anything with the Kicks. Not your run-down field, your coach who is more like a babysitter, or your gross uniforms. It's only the best for the Panthers."

She turned and swept out of the store, her head held high.

"Good riddance," Jessi muttered.

"Wow, Jessi." Emma shook her head. "I can't believe you said that!"

"It was kind of mean," Zoe agreed.

But Frida stuck up for Jessi. "Are you guys totally forgetting how awful Mirabelle was to all of us? She had it coming. And besides, she totally just put down the Kicks—*again*!"

Emma nodded. "I know our uniforms aren't as fancy as the Panthers', but I don't think they are gross!"

"And it totally wasn't cool of her to trash Coach Flores," Zoe said. "Coach is always so nice to everyone. She was even nice to Mirabelle!"

Jessi sighed. "I know, and I probably shouldn't have started with her. But seeing her at the game the other day brought back all those bad memories of how she treated us—and especially me, after our friendship breakup."

"You're better off without her," I said as I slung an arm around Jessi's shoulder. "Besides, you've got us now!"

"True." Jessi's face brightened. "And I'm with my new best friends in the mall, and the best part is yet to come."

"Best part?" Zoe asked.

"Boys and pizza!" Jessi said, pointing her finger toward the ceiling. "To the third floor!"

I laughed. "What, do they have a store on the third floor where they sell boys and pizza?"

"What do they call it, Boys R Us?" Emma joked.

"Or maybe they call it Cody Hut," Zoe said with a sly smile at Jessi.

Jessi looked a little embarrassed at Zoe's comment, but she tried to laugh it off. "Whatever. The arcade is on the third floor, and that's where all the boys hang out. The food court's on the third floor too. So let's go check it out!"

We followed her out of the store and up the escalator.

The smells of the food court hit us as we headed across the mall. Just as Jessi had said, a bunch of boys were hanging out talking in front of the arcade.

"So, um, what are we supposed to do?" I asked. "Talk to them?"

"No. We just watch them and decide who's cute," Jessi replied. "Wait, is that Brendan Insler over there?"

Zoe blushed. "No, thank goodness. What did Frida tell you?"

"Only that he follows you around like a puppy and carries your books everywhere now," Jessi answered.

"I never said he was like a puppy," Frida protested. "Although, that's not a bad description."

"Right. A sweaty, annoying puppy," Zoe said, making a face.

"Hey, I think there's some soccer boys over there," I said, pointing. "Isn't that Cody and Steven?"

"Don't point!" Jessi said frantically, pushing down my arm, but it was too late. Cody waved at us with a big smile on his face, and Steven gave us kind of a shy wave.

I waved back, but Jessi grabbed me by the arm and started pulling me toward the food court. The other girls followed us.

"What was that about?" I asked.

"You can't point like that!" Jessi cried. "Then they'll think we like them."

"But you *do* like Cody, don't you?" I asked.

Jessi rolled her eyes. "That is totally not the point."

"I'm hungry," Emma said. "Let's get that pizza."

Frida closed her eyes. "Mmm, pizza."

"Are you going to order yours with an extra topping of Cody?" I couldn't help but tease Jessi, who glared at me.

"Shhhh! He might hear you," Jessi said nervously, glancing back at the arcade.

"We're in the crowded, noisy mall, totally across the room from him," I reminded her. I was starting to think that when Cody was around, Jessi's brain short-circuited or something.

"Unless he has some kind of superhero hearing or something," Emma said, and giggled.

"Jessi thinks he's got some superpowers, that's for sure." Zoe grinned.

"Maybe his superpower is kissing," Frida said. She folded her hands across her chest and began puckering her lips, making loud smacking noises as she kissed the air. "I'm Cody," she said in between air kisses. "Or you can call me by my secret identity superhero name, Captain Kiss!"

"Frida!" Jessi shrieked, and lunged at her. Frida took off running, with Jessi in hot pursuit.

Emma, Zoe, and I exchanged glances and then started cracking up, laughing so hard I thought I was going to cry.

Frida came back, panting hard, and hid behind me as Jessi went to grab her.

"Truce!" I yelled, putting my hands in the air to stop Jessi. "We're starving. Let's go eat some pizza. And, Frida, knock off the Captain Kiss."

As soon as I said that, everyone started laughing again, even Jessi this time. It just sounded so ridiculous.

"Frida," I said as the laughter died down, "for your next role at a soccer game, all I think you need to do is pretend Jessi is chasing you. I've never seen you run so fast!"

"Or maybe," Frida said with a gleam in her eyes, "I could play Captain Kiss's loyal sidekick, Lip Stick."

"Frida!" Jessi yelled as she jumped at her, while Frida laughed and raced away again.

I shook my head. My friends might have been crazy, but they definitely made life interesting.

CHAPTER FIVE

"Devin, stop yawning!" Kara pleaded. "Now you're making *me* yawn!"

Kara had gotten special permission from her parents to stay up late Friday night so we wouldn't miss our webcam session. It was eight p.m. for me when I called her, but it was eleven p.m. in Connecticut.

"Sorry," I said. "It's been a crazy week. First my uniform got stolen, and then Zoe got hurt, and then I tried out some new positions at practice, and it was a disaster. And I had a vocab test in the middle of this, and then we went to the mall tonight. . . ."

"Sounds like you need to relax," Kara remarked.

"No way!" I replied. "There's practice tomorrow."

"We've got practice tomorrow too," Kara began. "And—"

"Afterward I want to research more drills for the next time I get to run practice," I continued, too focused on my plans for practice to really listen to Kara.

Kara's blue eyes got wide. "Whoa, are you totally obsessing on the team, or what?" She sounded a little annoyed.

"That's what Jessi and everyone else keeps saying to me," I replied. I thought Kara, out of everybody, would understand. "You know we've both been dreaming about becoming professional soccer players ever since second grade. Except when you went through that phase of wanting to be a cowgirl."

Kara laughed. "I still have the hat and boots, although they are way too small for me now."

I nodded. "Well, it's just that I keep thinking if I really want to go pro, I need to start now. And being on a championship team will totally help when it's time to apply for colleges."

"College is a long way off," Kara reminded me. "We're only in middle school. Don't forget the reason we both dream about being pro soccer players is because of how much fun we have playing. It doesn't sound like fun to be yawning on the field all the time."

Saying that, she let out a big yawn and frowned. "Rats! I made myself yawn that time."

"My bed is calling me," I said. "See you tomorrow night."

"See ya!"

I was always a little sad when the screen went dark after our chats, but I was seriously tired. When I woke up at eight the next morning, I felt supercharged and ready for practice. I raced down the stairs.

"Want some pancakes?" my dad asked, sitting at the kitchen table, drinking a cup of coffee.

"What Devin needs is some complex carbs for energy before practice," Mom told him. "How about some granola cereal with a banana and a glass of OJ?" she asked me.

Whew, close one! I'd thought she was going to offer me one of her green smoothies. The granola cereal was way yummier, so I happily agreed.

When Dad dropped me off at the field, I jogged out of the car, feeling like I needed to do five laps around just to get going. But I took only a few steps before I realized that the field was occupied by a bunch of senior citizens. Puzzled, I jogged up to Coach Flores.

"What are they doing here? Are they almost done?" I asked anxiously.

"Actually, they just started," Coach replied. "Apparently they had the field scheduled for the morning, which is very odd, because the community center knows we get the field every Saturday at this time unless we have a game."

"Can't we ask them to leave?" I asked, but I knew what Coach would say. She was way too nice to kick a bunch of old people off a field.

"I don't have the heart," Coach replied, just as I had guessed.

"You know, it's so unfair that we have to use the community field anyway," I said. "Why do the boys always get the good field? We're both winning now. We should split it up or something."

Coach Flores nodded. "I've been lobbying the school's athletic director for a new field for us, so maybe we'll get some good news soon," she answered. "And today's not totally lost either. Mrs. Tanaka, the teacher, said that we could join her class, and I think it's a wonderful idea; tai chi can help with coordination and focus."

My mom did yoga and tai chi, so I was kind of familiar with it. It was invented in China, and it was this series of slow, precise movements—kind of like kung fu in slow motion. But I definitely didn't feel like moving in slow motion this morning.

The rest of the players started to arrive, and confusion quickly broke out, until Coach Flores explained the situation. Some of the girls were happy about doing tai chi.

"I saw this on *The Real Teenagers of Beverly Hills*," Jessi told me. "Belinda took a class after her pet psychic said her Yorkipoo was picking up on her nervous energy."

"That sounds nuts!" I said. "Besides, I thought you gave up on those trashy reality shows."

"I watch them only after I've done all my homework and studying," Jessi said. "It's like my reward for working hard. Anyway, Belinda said tai chi is very relaxing. Her Yorkipoo agreed. According to the pet psychic, anyway."

"We're not supposed to be relaxing. We're supposed to be practicing," I complained.

Emma gave me a little push from behind. "I think some relaxing is just what you need this morning, Devin!"

It was no use fighting it; we spent an hour doing tai

chi on the field with the seniors. I guess I could see how it could be relaxing, but all I could think about was that we had a game against the Santa Flora Roses the next morning, and we were moving in slow motion instead of practicing. Aargh!

I'd been hoping we could practice after the tai chi was over, but some guys from an adult baseball league showed up and we had to leave.

"What about tomorrow, Coach?" I asked. "Tomorrow's game is on the home field, so maybe we could get there an hour early for a little extra warm-up time."

"I don't see why not," Coach answered, and then she turned to the rest of the team. "Let's report to the main field tomorrow at ten, okay? Oh, and don't forget glow bowling tonight!"

Everyone cheered. Coach Flores liked doing team building exercises with us, and the glow-in-the-dark bowling sounded like fun. I had never done it, but I was really curious to try.

I walked up to Jessi. "So, what are you doing until we go bowling?"

"Want to study math with me?" Jessi asked. "Mom said if you come over, she'll make us lunch."

"Just as long as it's not tuna casserole," I said.

Jessi looked at me like I was crazy. "Why would my mom make you tuna casserole?" she asked.

I shook my head and laughed. "Long story. But, yes, I'll do math with you. Let me go home and change, and I'll see if my mom or dad will drive me."

I got to Jessi's house about an hour later. Jessi came outside to meet me. Her dad was in the front yard, pruning some bushes. I'd met him only a couple of times before because he worked a lot, but he seemed nice. He was a big guy with a friendly smile like Jessi's.

"Hey there, Devin," he said. "Jessi tells me you had an interesting practice this morning."

"It was very relaxing," Jessi said, grinning at me.

"You mean boring," I corrected her.

Jessi nodded toward the door. "Mom made us some lunch."

She led me inside, and we found the kitchen table set for us with tuna salad sandwiches and carrot sticks.

"I hope tuna sandwiches are okay," Jessi said apologetically.

"Definitely," I replied. "They're, like, in a whole different food category from casseroles."

Jessi's mom walked in and gave me a big smile. "Thanks so much for helping Jessi with her math today, Devin," Mrs. Dukes said. She was wearing her hair in braids like Jessi was, but you could tell that Jessi was going to be taller than her soon. "Jessi's grades are improving every day."

Not too long ago, Jessi had been failing math and Spanish, and her mom had taken her off the team. Thankfully, Jessi had started studying hard and Mrs. Dukes had let her back on the team, and I helped Jessi study whenever I could.

"Well, I'll be out in the garden if you need me," Mrs. Dukes said, and then she headed into the backyard.

Jessi and I ate our sandwiches, and Jessi was chatting a mile a minute about how she wanted to go back to the mall to get this shirt she'd seen in a magazine, and how there'd been a big fight between Belinda's and Julianna's pet psychics on *The Real Teenagers of Beverly Hills*, but I wasn't really listening. I couldn't stop thinking about the goof-up over the field that morning. Our team always practiced there. It didn't make any sense. While Jessi talked, I did that thing where you just said "Mmm-hmm" and "Yeah" and nodded your head every few seconds. Then Jessi's voice broke through my fog.

"Devin? Are you listening?"

"Oh, sorry," I replied. "I'm still upset that we missed practice this morning. The whole thing about the wrong schedule is bugging me. I should call over to the community center and make sure our next practice is scheduled. Do you mind?"

Jessi shook her head. "Fine. Do whatever you need to do to clear that head of yours!"

I looked up the number on my cell phone and then called the center. Luckily, somebody picked up on the first ring.

"Hi, um, I'm wondering about the schedule for the field on King Street," I said. "There was a mix-up this morning with our soccer practice, and I just want to make sure we're still scheduled for Monday afternoon."

"Give me a second," said the female voice on the other end, and I heard the sound of shuffling papers. "Let me see . . . It doesn't look like there was a mix-up. Coach Flores called yesterday to cancel the use of the field for the Kicks."

"Coach Flores?" I asked, shocked. "I saw Coach Flores this morning, and she was just as surprised as everyone else that the field was being used by the tai chi group. I'm sure she never called, I swear."

"I'm sorry, but that's what I have here," the woman said. "Is there anything else I can help you with?"

"No, no," I said, frustrated. "Just please don't cancel any more of our dates, okay?"

I hung up, upset, and Jessi was looking at me strangely. "What was that?"

"Somebody claiming to be Coach Flores called the center and canceled this morning's practice," I told her, and her mouth dropped open.

"No way!" she cried. "Devin, don't you see? Somebody is definitely trying to sabotage our team. This can't be a coincidence."

I frowned. "Jessi, that sounds crazy. Who would want to do that?"

"Mirabelle!" she shot back. "I've been thinking about it. Mirabelle hated being on the Kicks because she thought we were losers. When she went to the Panthers, she thought she'd be on the top team in the league, and then we beat them. She's probably trying to make sure we don't win."

"That sounds drastic, even for Mirabelle," I said.

"Think about it," Jessi said, her eyes shining with excitement. "Mirabelle was at the game the day your uniform was stolen. She knows the locker room well. So she calls the office pretending to be your mom. You go to the office, and she sneaks in and grabs the duffel bag. She knew it would throw you off your game."

I nodded, thinking. Jessi was actually kind of making sense.

"I also asked Coach Flores about the e-mail. You know, the one telling the girls that practice was moved up?" Jessi asked. "She said she never had the e-mail address coachflores@mailmee.us. Not ever! Someone created that e-mail address to send out the fake e-mails, I just know it!"

I had to agree with Jessi that that seemed really fishy.

"And now somebody called the community center pretending to be Coach and canceled our practice," Jessi continued. "Mirabelle knows that we practice on the community field, not the school field. It *had* to be her. I bet the reason Zoe got hurt is her fault too."

"Now you're being ridiculous," I argued. "Zoe and Brianna bumped into each other. That wasn't sabotage."

"Okay, maybe not," Jessi admitted. "But your duffel bag and the field—come on. Something bad is going on here."

I still didn't want to believe it. "We've got to forget about this stuff and just concentrate on the game against the Roses tomorrow."

"Well, *I'm* not forgetting," Jessi said, and she looked more determined than I'd ever seen her. "If Mirabelle is behind this, there is no way she's going to get away with it."

"Yay! Devin's here!" Emma squealed as I walked into Cosmic Bowling later that night. She slipped a blue fluorescent necklace over my head. "Coach Flores got us these. Aren't they cool?"

"Awesome!" I replied. I scanned the bowling alley, transfixed. The room was bathed in black light. The bowling pins and balls glowed in fluorescent green, yellow, orange, and pink. Bowlers wore glow-in-the-dark necklaces and bracelets, and people even sipped sodas from glow-in-the-dark straws. I had never seen anything like it.

"Where is everybody?" I asked.

"We've all got lanes," Emma reported. "Come on. We need to get you some shoes."

A few minutes later I was walking through the bowling alley in smooth-soled bowling shoes. Emma led me to a lane where Jessi, Frida, and Zoe were all waiting.

"I can't bowl, but I can cheer everybody on," Zoe said, wiggling her arm like a chicken wing.

"Aw!" I said, hugging her. "Well, I'm going to need a lot of cheering on, because the last time I bowled, I used bumpers."

"You mean we can't use bumpers?"

Anna, another member of the Kicks, had asked the question. She was in the lane to the right of us with Sarah.

Jessi made a muscle with her right arm. "We don't need no stinkin' bumpers!"

"Speak for yourself," I said.

Brianna ran up, carrying her bowling shoes. She plopped down in a seat next to me.

"Sorry I'm late. I had a piano lesson," she said.

"I thought you had a dance lesson today," Anna said.

"I did," Brianna replied. "Right after soccer practice." She swept a lock of her long blond hair behind her ear. "Oh, that reminds me. You know Jamie from the Rams? Well, she's in my dance class and all she could talk about was how the Rams are going to win the district this year. It was obnoxious."

"She thinks the Rams can beat the Panthers?" Jessi asked. "Aren't the Rams, like, in fourth place right now or something?"

"Well, *we* beat the Panthers, and I think we're in fifth place right now," I pointed out.

"I know," Brianna said. Then she rolled her eyes. "That Jamie was acting like they'd already won."

"Well, the Rams did really well last year," Emma pointed out. "Jamie was, like, the star of the team. It's actually kind of weird that they're not doing better this year."

Then Coach Flores walked up to us. "Glad to see all of you girls here! It looks like most of the team made it."

I looked at the lanes around us. To our left were Grace and her three best friends on the team, Giselle, Megan, and Anjali. The other girls on the team were all in lanes close by.

"Are you bowling too?" I asked Coach.

She nodded to a lane. "Maya and Jade invited me to play

with them. But I'll stop by to see how you guys are doing."

I shook my head. "You might not want to do that. I haven't bowled in ages. So I'll probably just be throwing gutter balls."

Coach Flores smiled. "Just have some fun. I'll see you later!"

She left, and I looked up at the scoreboard screen to see that Jessi had entered our names. Then she picked up a glowing pink ball.

"Let's roll!" she yelled, and then she sent the ball sailing down the lane and knocked down a bunch of pins.

"Whoo!" she cheered, and Emma gave her a high five.

Jessi, Emma, and Frida had to go before me, so I looked around at the other bowlers. Anna pushed the ball with both hands, giggling as it slowly made its way down the side of the lane before dropping into the gutter. The eighth grade lane was another story. Grace slid up to the line like a real pro and sent her ball spinning right down the middle. She pumped her fist as the word "Strike" blazed across the scoreboard.

"Devin, it's your turn," Emma called out.

"Oh, boy," I muttered. I wasn't nervous, exactly, just not sure how I was going to do. I picked up a fluorescent orange ball and walked up to the line. Then I swung with all my might and dropped the ball. It quickly skidded down the lane—and right into the gutter.

Secretly I was embarrassed, but I decided to make the best of it.

"Yes!" I cheered, pumping my fist like Grace had. "I totally meant to do that!"

Zoe giggled. "That was the most awesome gutter ball ever."

The ball came back, and I tried again, this time focusing as hard as I could on the middle pin. But the ball rolled right into the gutter again!

"Thank you, thank you," I said, taking a bow.

"Devin is the gutter ball queen!" Frida yelled.

"No way! I am!" Anna protested.

"We'll see about that," I said.

On my next turn I danced up to the line to the music and then threw the ball—another gutter ball, but I didn't care, because my friends were giggling so hard. I hopped up to the line like a bunny on my second throw.

I mixed it up on each turn, cracking up my friends every time. I twirled around like a ballerina. I stomped like a sumo wrestler. I swung my arms like a monkey. And the ball went into the gutter every time.

"Enough!" Jessi yelled finally through her giggles. "Devin, you have got to hit at least one pin this game!"

"Pretend the ball is a soccer ball and the pins are the goal," Frida suggested.

"Okay, okay," I said. I picked up the ball, and this time I really tried. I took Frida's advice. The glowing orange ball became a black-and-white soccer ball. The fluorescent pins became goalposts and a net. I took three smooth steps, like I had seen Jessi and Grace do, and let go of the ball.

It slid down the middle . . . and kept going . . . and then veered to the left right before it hit the pins.

Bam! Four pins went down.

"I did it!" I cried, and Emma gave me another high five.

I knew it was only four pins, but at least it wasn't a gutter ball. Jessi shook her head.

"It's a good thing you're a better soccer player than a bowler," she said.

I laughed. "No kidding!"

CHAPTER SIX

The next morning Dad dropped me off early at the Santa Flora field for our game against the Roses. Santa Flora was only one town away from Kentville, so it wasn't far. It looked like a pretty normal school field except that there were rosebushes planted all around the parking lot, which was really pretty.

I walked to the Kicks side of the field, where some of the girls were already warming up. Coach Flores approached me.

"Devin, Grace, and Megan are both out today with a stomach bug," she informed me. "But we've got plenty of players, so we should be fine."

I couldn't answer her right away, because I was kind of freaking out inside. Fine? Grace was our strongest mid-fielder, and Megan, who was also in eighth grade, was a solid striker. Now we'd have a forward line without Megan *or* Zoe. Not good.

"Okay," I said finally. "So, what are you going to do, Coach?"

"I thought I'd start you, Brianna, and Maya as forwards," Coach Flores replied. "Maya's a great midfielder, but I think she'll do well in the forward position."

I couldn't really argue with that; Maya was another eighth grader and I didn't know her that well, but she was definitely solid on the midfield. Still, I didn't feel like it was our strongest front line.

"Coach, could we put Jessi as a forward too?" I asked.

Coach Flores raised an eyebrow. "You mean four forwards? I wouldn't normally recommend that, Devin."

"I just think we need to beef up our front line," I said. "It's worth a try, isn't it? I mean, we've tried stuff before that has worked."

Coach Flores nodded. "They say the best way to learn is by doing, right? Let's give it a try."

By now most of the team had showed up, and Coach explained the new formation. When she finished, I yelled out, "Sock swap!" All of us gathered in a circle, took off one of the colorful, crazy socks we were wearing, and handed it to the person on our left. Then we put on our socks and our cleats and were ready to go. Coach Flores led us in some warm-ups and drills. Before long, spectators began to fill the stands, and the Santa Flora Roses showed up in their red-and-white uniforms.

I wasn't too worried about the Roses. They'd had almost as many losses as we had, although theirs had been spread out a little more over the season. But we still had to win this game to stay in the running for the play-offs.

We had retreated to the sidelines to get ready for the start, when Jessi poked my arm.

"Cody and Steven are up there," she told me in a loud whisper. "Just don't point this time!"

I followed her gaze and saw Cody and Steven in the stands with some of the other players from the boys' team. Steven saw me and waved, and I smiled and waved back.

"What are you doing?" Jessi hissed.

"I'm waving, not pointing," I protested, but then I quickly turned away from the stands. Waving at Steven was *not* a good way to get focused before a game.

Frida ran up. "So what's my motivation today?"

"I've got one," Jessi offered. "You're a military operative guarding a top secret base, and inside the soccer ball is a secret spy camera. If the ball gets into the goal, your enemy will learn all the details of your secret base."

Frida made a really serious face. "Military. Got it." She saluted and then marched away just as the ref's whistle blew. I ran out onto the field for the coin toss, and the Roses won, which meant they would start with control of the ball. Both teams spread out on the field, and Jessi, Brianna, Maya, and I took our places on the forward line. The ref blew his whistle again, and the Roses charged forward.

Right from the start we were in trouble. I thought having four forwards would be good, but it caused us a lot of problems. For one, it meant that we had only three midfielders on the field—Alandra, Taylor, and Anna. They were the ones who did the most running on the field, because they were in a position to defend the goal from the opposing players, as well as trying to get the ball up to the forwards. It was a lot of ground to cover, and the three of them got tired out quickly, so the Roses offense got past them pretty easily and kept breezing past our defenders.

"The spy camera is about to infiltrate headquarters!" Frida yelled as the ball whizzed past her. The Roses midfielder chasing after the ball looked at her quizzically as she passed, but that didn't stop her from shooting the ball past Emma and into the net.

"I have failed!" Frida cried dramatically, dropping to her knees.

"Don't give up hope!" Emma called back. "Hold that line. I'm counting on you, Agent Frida!"

Frida saluted. "I won't fail again."

But the tired midfielders couldn't hold off the onslaught of the Roses' offense. One of their strikers tore down toward the goal. Frida, Anjali, and Sarah all converged toward her, but she kicked it right past them. Emma dove for it, and her fingers brushed it, but she couldn't stop it.

"Nooooo!" Emma wailed.

The Roses had scored two goals in ten minutes. After

the second goal Coach switched out Anna for Gabriela, one of the eighth grade players, and that helped for a little bit. But then when the midfielders passed the ball up to the forwards, things got confusing. At one point Alandra sent the ball skidding across the grass up the middle of the field, and Jessi and I charged toward it at the same time. At the last second I remembered the Zoe-Brianna crash and I stopped short—and Jessi did the same. One of the Roses forwards swooped in and got control of the ball for their team.

Maya got the ball a couple of times, but while she was petite and full of energy like Zoe, she had more stamina than speed. She couldn't zigzag her way through the Roses midfielders the way Zoe could. At one point one of the Roses midfielders got the ball and dribbled it all the way up the left flank, which was wide open because Gabriela couldn't get to her in time. The Roses midfielder kicked the ball hard and high past Frida on the defense line, and my heart sank as it looked like the ball would fly right into the goal. Then Emma jumped up and swatted it away—but still, it was a close call.

Coach Flores took advantage of the break and called Maya off the field.

"Olivia, play midfield!" I heard her yell, but Olivia must have gotten confused, because she thought she was supposed to replace Maya, so she ran up to the forward line. For the last five minutes of the first half, the Roses kept getting past the midfielders again and again.

Finally the first half ended. I ran up to Coach Flores, panting a little.

"So I guess that was a bad idea," I admitted.

"Well, now we know," Coach said with a sympathetic smile. "So let's try something different in the next half, okay?"

I nodded. "Definitely."

I kind of felt bad about how the first half had gone down, so I stepped back a little and let Coach Flores run things. We went back to a pretty standard three-four-three formation (three defenders, four midfielders, three forwards). She put Maya back in the midfield with Anna, who'd sat out most of the first half and was pretty fresh; Jade, who normally played defense; and Taylor. Anjali, Sarah, and Giselle played defense, and Coach kept me, Jessi, and Brianna as forwards. Emma was exhausted from defending so many goals, so Coach put Zarine on the goal. This made me a little bit nervous until I remembered how well Zarine had performed during the shoot-out drill.

Frida marched up to me and saluted. "I failed in my mission, Colonel," she said, hanging her head. "It's up to you now to keep the base safe. The fate of the world is in your hands."

"You can count on me," I said in my best serious voice, but I wasn't an actress like Frida, and I started cracking up.

It might have seemed like a small change to add one more player to the midfield, but it was exactly what we needed to recover. The Roses had a much harder time getting past our midfielders, and we got a lot more passes from the midfielders than before.

The first one came from Maya to Jessi, who zipped past a Roses defender and sent the ball wailing over the goalie's head. We had scored—in the first minute of the half!

Maya and Jessi high-fived.

"Nice pass!" Jessi said.

Maya grinned. "Nice goal!"

Sometimes it amazed me how things could turn around when all seemed hopeless. Once you got momentum going, it raised the energy level of the whole team. Taylor intercepted a pass from one of the Roses midfielders and sent it my way. I had to chase it a little bit, but once I was on it, I kept the ball close. All three of the Roses defenders ran up to stop me, so I quickly looked to my right and saw I had a clear path to Jessi; I sent her a lateral pass, and luckily, she saw it coming. She stopped the ball and then charged forward as the Roses defenders scrambled to block her.

Whoosh! She sent another ball sailing over the goalie's head.

I ran up and slapped her hand. "You are on fire!" I told her, and Jessi grinned.

I scored a goal after that, and Brianna scored one too, making it Kicks 4, Roses 2. During one weak moment in the Kicks' defense, a Roses midfielder made an amazing drive down the side of the field and sent a ball whizzing into the corner of the goal, out of Zarine's reach. But that was the Roses' last point. We ended the game 4–3 and lined up to shake the hands of the Roses.

When I got to the end of the line, the captain smiled at me. She was a tall girl who wore her hair in a ponytail.

"Thanks for being nice about it," she said. "When we played the Rams, they didn't even shake our hands. They pretended to, but then they pulled their hands away at the last second."

"Really?" I asked.

She nodded. "I know. Rude, right? Their captain, Jamie, is the worst one. She fouled me, like, three times."

I jogged back to the sideline, shaking my head. We still hadn't faced the Rams yet, and I wasn't looking forward to it.

"Great game, everybody!" Coach Flores called out.

"She means 'great second half,'" Emma said as we gathered up our equipment. "I thought we were going to lose this one."

"You did an amazing job in the first half," I told her. "You let only two goals past you. That made it easier for us to catch up."

Emma grinned. "Thanks!"

After a brief talk from Coach we left the field. Cody and Steven were hanging out by the fence, so we had to walk past them, and I couldn't help wondering if they had put themselves there on purpose.

Steven smiled at me again. "Good game."

"Thanks," I replied, and suddenly all I could think about was Kara singing, "Devin and Steven." I could feel my cheeks get warm.

"That was a little crazy there in the beginning," Cody remarked. "Leaving your midfield open like that."

I blushed even harder; the whole thing had been kind of embarrassing. "Well, Zoe's still out, and Grace and Megan were out today, so we were trying to compensate for losing some of our strongest players."

"Guess that didn't work out so well," Steven said with a grin, and there was nothing mean about the way he said it, so I laughed.

"No, I guess not." Then I realized that both boys were in uniform. "Are you guys playing today?"

Steven nodded. "Our game's next."

"Yeah, Devin and I were going to stay and watch," Jessi said.

I looked at Jessi. "We were?" I asked, and she gave me a look.

"Oh, yeah," I said. "We were. I just need to, um, check in with my parents."

Jessi and I quickly walked to the stands, and I started giggling. "Why did you say that?"

"Come on. It'll be fun," Jessi said. "They watched our game, so it's the nice thing to do."

I raised an eyebrow. "And it has nothing to do with your crush on Cody?"

"Maybe . . . ," Jessi said slowly. "Anyway, we won! So think of it as a celebration."

"Definitely!" I agreed, and a wave of relief swept over me. Despite a terrible first half, we had recovered, which meant we were one step closer to the play-offs.

CHAPTER SEVEN

Jessi and I headed to the stands and found our parents, who were making their way to the exit together, talking and laughing. I guess they were starting to become friends since Jessi and I had become friends, which was kind of nice.

"It looks like the Kicks are on the Play-offs Express with no exits!" Dad joked when he saw me.

"I sure hope so!" I smiled. "Hey, do you think it would be okay if Jessi and I stayed to watch the boys' game?"

My mom and dad exchanged glances and nodded. "That should be fine, honey," my mom answered. "We'll pick you up on our way back from getting Maisie. She's having a playdate at Riley's house."

Then she turned to Mrs. Dukes. "We could give Jessi a ride home."

"That would be great," Jessi's mom replied. "I've got to bake a bunch of cookies for the bake sale tomorrow, and Jerry's got to go back to his office for a few hours."

I gave Mom a hug. "Thanks! We'll see you later."

Before we could step away, my mom handed me a water bottle. "You played hard; you need to replace the fluids you lost," she said seriously.

"Mom, I have so many fluids in me, I could fill a swimming pool!" I said. "Seriously, I'm practically floating out on the field."

"Then my work here is done," Mom said smugly, but with a smile.

Jessi and I headed to the part of the stands where the kids always hung out, and we got ready to support our fellow Kangaroos. Emma and Zoe were already there and waved to us.

"You guys are staying too?" I asked.

"Sure, it should be a good game," Emma replied. "The boys' team is awesome."

"Well, most of the boys' team," Jessi said, and we all knew what she meant. After we'd had our disastrous loss against Pinewood, some of the boys—led by the eighth grade captain, Trey Bishop—had completely embarrassed us in front of everybody at the school dance. They'd called us losers while Mirabelle, our own teammate at the time, had laughed. It had been the lowest of the low points for the Kicks.

"Well, maybe, but they made it up to us with that pizza

party," Emma reminded us. "And they even apologized."

"Well, I need something to take my mind off my wrist," Zoe added. "It is such a pain! And it's so boring not to be able to play. I can't wait until I can get back on the field."

"Me too," I agreed. "Hey, where's Frida?"

"Some acting class thing," Zoe replied. Then the boys' team ran onto the field, and everybody stood up and clapped.

"We're blue, we're white, we're ready to fight," Emma cheered. "We're white, we're blue, we'll stomp all over you! Goooooo, Kangaroos!"

"Look! The game is starting!" Jessi interrupted. "I bet Cody is going to do great."

I let that go by without a comment. I didn't want to tease Jessi anymore about her crush on Cody, because I didn't want to get teased in return. I still didn't really know how I felt about Steven; he was super nice and cute, but it was all so confusing.

It was much more fun to get into the game on the field, anyway. The Kangaroos were like an unstoppable blue-and-white wave, sweeping up and down the field and getting the first two goals of the game within minutes. Steven, a striker, made the second one.

"Way to go!" I gave an extra loud cheer. I couldn't help it. It just popped out! Jessi looked at me with an eyebrow raised, but I ignored her.

The Roses managed to get it together and pushed back, moving the ball fluidly and connecting passes. One of the

Roses stole the ball from a Kangaroos defender and fed it to a Roses striker, who passed it across the goal. The action was intense, and we all had our eyes glued to the field the entire time.

At the beginning of the second half the teams were tied up. The Kangaroos had control of the ball. Michael, a midfielder, swung back his leg, ready to give the ball a hard smack toward Cody. But when his foot connected, the ball exploded! The black inner lining oozed out of the top, making the ball look like a fat bowling pin.

Michael watched the ball as it rolled listlessly for a few short feet before stopping. He grabbed it and with a bemused smile threw it to the referee, who called time. While the players waited for a new ball and the game to resume, Jessi turned to me, Emma, and Zoe and motioned for us to get close.

"Sabotage!" she said in a loud whisper, her eyes wide. I felt her fingers digging into my skin.

"Ouch!" I said, shaking her hand off, before rubbing my arm. "Jessi, you've got to relax."

She pointed a finger at me. "Mark my words. Something funny is going on. And I want to know what it is!"

"I think Jessi's right," Emma agreed. "There are too many weird things happening."

"Yeah, like who's ever heard of a soccer ball exploding?" Zoe asked.

"Soccer balls explode sometimes," I said, although I really wasn't sure. To be honest, all the sabotage talk was making me nervous. I didn't want the team to lose focus on our upcoming games.

"It can't just be a coincidence," Jessi pressed on.

"Then who did it?" I asked. "If it's Mirabelle, why would she sabotage the boys' team? She doesn't care about them, does she?"

"Well, maybe she . . . ," Jessi began, but her voice trailed off.

Then the crowd burst into a cheer and we turned our attention back to the field. Cody had control of the new ball and was furiously dribbling toward the goal. A Roses defender got in front of him, but Cody body-faked the defender, acting like he was crossing right for the ball, when in reality he let it roll to his left. That gave him space to send a hard shot to Steven. I held my breath as Steven kicked it hard and over the goalie's head . . . right into the goal!

We all leaped to our feet, clapping and shouting at the spectacular goal. The Roses lost momentum after that, and the Kangaroos won the game, 3–2. It looked like both the girls' and boys' Kangaroos were on the Play-offs Express!

When I woke up the next morning, my usual morning text from Kara was waiting for me.

Blue button-up shirt, skinny jeans, ballet flats w/ bows. Wish I could wear flip-flops too, but it's getting cold here!

I looked at the attached photo and at Kara's grinning face, her long, brown hair pulled into a ponytail with a cute ribbon. When I'd lived in Connecticut, Kara and I had always picked out our school outfits together. With a three-hour time difference and a totally different climate, that had become impossible. But I was so glad we kept the tradition as much as we could. As soon as I got dressed, I snapped a pic of myself and sent it to her:

Layered blue and orange tanks, jeans, and of course flip-flops :)

What people wore at Kentville Middle School was a lot different from the preppy Connecticut school I had gone to, but I found myself liking the relaxed Cali style.

Jessi, Zoe, Emma, and I sat in the courtyard behind the library at lunch, in our usual spot. (Frida sat with us sometimes, but mostly she hung with her drama club friends.) The sky was bright blue and the sun was shining, with big, fluffy white clouds dotting the sky. I thought of the cool, autumn air that was descending on Connecticut (and Kara!) right then and shivered. California definitely had its perks!

I had just finished the yogurt parfait my mom had packed for me and was licking the spoon (it was so delish!) when Jessi pulled me aside.

"Devin, come with?" she asked.

"Where?" I said nervously. She had that I'm-up-to-something look in her eyes.

"I want to go to the cafeteria to find Cody and Steven," she said. "As Kangaroos I think they need to know that someone has been targeting the Kicks. And now it looks as if the boys' team is in danger too!"

Boy, and I thought Frida was the dramatic one. But I could tell there would be no point in arguing with Jessi. It would just be easier to get it over with.

"Fine," I sighed as I slowly got to my feet. Emma and Zoe were deep in conversation about a social studies project they were working on together and barely noticed we were leaving.

We walked through the crowded cafeteria and found Cody and Steven eating with a bunch of the other boy soccer players.

"Hey, can we talk to you guys alone?" Jessi asked, her hands on her hips.

"Oooooooooooh," one of the boys at the table called out, while another made kissing noises.

"Oh, grow up," Jessi said with an eye roll.

But Cody just laughed. "Sure," he said, while Steven gave me a grin and a wave.

We walked over to an empty table in the very back of the cafeteria, and before we even had our butts in the chairs, Jessi launched into it.

"The Kicks are being sabotaged and we think someone is after your team too!" she said urgently.

"What?" Cody asked, surprised, while Steven's eyes grew wide.

Jessi outlined everything that had happened so far: the fake e-mail from Coach Flores, the stolen duffel bag, and the canceled practice.

"And then at your game against the Roses, the exploding

soccer ball. When has that ever happened in all the years you've played soccer?" she asked. "Someone is out to get us. And I'm pretty sure that someone is the Pinewood Panthers." She leaned back in her chair and looked expectantly at Cody, waiting for him to see her point.

But instead Cody opened his mouth and started to laugh, like someone had told him a really funny joke. Jessi looked angry.

"The Panthers aren't even in the picture this year, not after their last couple of games," Cody said once he'd stopped chuckling. "The boys' team has zero chance of making it to the play-offs. So why would they try to take us out?"

Steven nodded. "Cody's right. Our main competition right now is the Rams."

"Yeah, and their girls' team is awesome too," Cody said. "Well, they were last year, anyway. Have you seen their captain, Jamie, play? She's so fast."

Jessi scowled, annoyed. "Everyone knows the Panthers-Kangaroos rivalry goes way back. And you remember what Mirabelle's like," Jessi insisted.

"Okay, say for a second it's true. That soccer ball bursting didn't even hurt us. We still won the game," Cody said. "Besides, I've heard that soccer balls explode sometimes."

"That's what I said," I chimed in.

Jessi placed her palms on the table and leaned toward Cody. "Don't you get it—they're mind games! They are meant to psych us out. When Devin's uniform was stolen, we didn't lose either. But it totally got under Devin's skin."

I blushed at that. I didn't want Steven to think I was easily rattled, but he gave me a sympathetic grin.

"But how would someone even do that to a soccer ball?" Cody shook his head. "It was just a freak accident."

"It happened right after halftime," Jessi said, not backing down. "Someone could have easily swapped one of the game balls with one that was rigged to go kablooey."

Cody laughed again. "Seriously, Jessi, I didn't think you were the type to go in for all this drama stuff."

Uh-oh, I thought. I nervously looked at Jessi, waiting for her to erupt. Her eyes flashed for a second. "Okay. Sorry to bother you," she said in a voice full of sarcasm.

She got up and stalked away from the table. I followed her. As I was leaving, Steven gave me another grin while shrugging his shoulders helplessly. That had not gone well.

As soon as we got out of the cafeteria, Jessi whirled around to face me. "And to think he wanted me to go to the fall carnival with him!" she huffed. "Well, he'd better think again now!"

"Wait. What fall carnival?" I asked.

Jessi sighed. "It's a big fund-raiser the middle school does every November. There are games, food, rides—it's really fun. A lot of boys and girls go together. You know, like on a date. Cody said that Steven might ask you and we could double-date."

Double-date? I gulped. I wasn't even sure how I felt

about Steven. And I had never been on a date in my life! I didn't know if my parents would let me go on a date or not.

Trying to make the play-offs. Schoolwork. The possibility (according to Jessi) that someone was trying to sabotage our teams. And now dating? It was all too much!

CHAPTER EIGHT

"He asked you on a date?" Kara shrieked over the webcam.

"No, he told Cody he *might*," I emphasized the word. It was a relief to talk to Kara. I felt like she was the only person in the world I could confide in about all this Steven stuff. Don't get me wrong. I was so glad I'd met Jessi, Emma, and Zoe, and they were awesome friends. But I'd known Kara for practically as long as I could remember. It just felt way too embarrassing to talk to the other Kicks about Steven.

Kara broke into her little "Devin and Steven" song. I had to admit, it was kind of catchy. She even got up and started doing a funny dance in front of the webcam. I started cracking up, and to encourage her to keep going, I started singing along. Loudly. So of course my dad picked that embarrassing moment to come into my bedroom!

"Devin, it's time for dinner," he said. Kara didn't hear

him and couldn't see him, so she kept on singing.

"So who exactly is this Steven?" Dad asked. He had a little grin on his face.

I quickly lowered the sound on my laptop. "Nothing! Nobody!" I replied.

On the screen I could see Kara mouthing my name, confused.

"Why don't you wrap up your call with Kara," he suggested. "And come downstairs and set the table."

"Okay, Dad," I turned the sound back up after he left. "My dad totally heard us!" I told Kara.

"Oops!" she laughed. "Oh my gosh, your face is so red!"

"I'm totally embarrassed," I groaned. "Whatever. I can't even think about this stuff right now. I'm going to stay focused on soccer, not Steven, until the season is over."

"Good luck with that!" Kara joked.

"Yeah, right," I said, laughing. I had a lot going on—school, friends, soccer, and the whole thing with Steven. Life was pretty complicated . . . but it was all good!

The next couple of days were a busy blur of school, soccer practice, and homework. I had a book to finish reading for English class, a ton of algebra homework, and a paper to write for science. We were studying Newton's laws of motion, so of course I had to relate it to soccer. My paper was about how the laws explained the movements of the soccer ball during a game, and it was by far my favorite homework assignment.

"Only Devin would turn science homework into a soccer project!" Jessi said at lunch that Wednesday. "Too bad they don't have a soccer class. Soccer 101. You'd get an A plus!"

Emma and Zoe laughed, and I joined in. I totally could not stop thinking about soccer, and my friends knew it. Every free second I could find, I spent thinking about the Kicks: How many more wins did we need to get us into the play-offs? Which teams needed to lose? What drills could we do at practice to strengthen us as a whole? What would be our best option for field positions to maximize our offensive line while Zoe was benched?

I put away my science paper and grabbed a printout from my folder. "Look at this shooting drill I found. It should really help strengthen our offense. I e-mailed it to Grace, and she likes it, so we're going to ask Coach if we can run it at practice today." After I'd finished my homework the night before, I'd spent the rest of the night looking up new drills on my computer.

Emma shook her head. "And I thought *I* loved soccer! Devin, you are obsessed!"

"Well, Devin's not the only obsessed one," Zoe said. "All I can think about is getting back on the field. The doctor says he might clear me to play next week."

Emma smiled. "Finally! We can be a complete team again," she said. "Hey, you know what? I saw the Kicks' state championship trophy from when Coach Flores was on the team. It's on a shelf in the hall by the library. It's really cool."

Jessi laughed. "Why did you tell Devin that? If she sees it, she'll just become even more obsessed!"

I laughed along with everyone else until I got the full impact of Jessi's words. Duh! I was so preoccupied that I had been overlooking one very important fact. The Kicks had been champions in the past. And our very own Coach Flores had been on that team. I needed to ask her, in detail, how they'd done it. Maybe someone had even videotaped their games, like my dad did with ours. My eyes lit up at the thought. I could study the videos to find ways to help the team!

After school that day I raced to Coach Flores's office, eager to talk to her before practice.

"Devin, what's up?" she asked as I came barreling into her office.

"Do you have any video recordings of your Kicks games?" I asked, panting.

"Whoa!" Coach said, laughing. "Relax. Have a seat and take a second to catch your breath."

I collapsed into the chair. I guess I had been a little overexcited.

"Do you mean from when I was a player on the Kicks?" Coach asked. I nodded, still panting.

"I do, and as a matter of fact, my father converted them from tapes to DVD a couple of years ago," Coach said. "I have them at home. Why?"

"I'd love to borrow some, to get some pointers, if that's okay," I replied.

"If you think it will help, sure," she said. But then her usual smile faded and she got a serious look on her face. "But remember, to achieve those results the coach had to be really tough on us, and we had to eat, sleep, and breathe soccer. I'm never going to be that kind of coach."

"I know, Coach. But it still could give us some great new ideas, right?" I said.

Coach Flores laughed. "Tell you what. I'll turn over my whistle to you and you can coach the team."

My eyes lit up, and she laughed even harder. "I was joking, Devin! Now relax, and remember to have fun! At the end of the day, it's only a game."

"Okay, I will," I said.

When I got to practice later that day, Coach had a surprise for me.

"I had to stop home anyway before practice today," she said, handing me a DVD case. "Here you go."

"Wow, thank you!" I cried, clutching the DVD like it was a valuable jewel or something. I couldn't wait to watch it!

After practice, homework, and dinner that night, I ran up to my room and stayed up late watching the champion Kicks' games until my dad shut off the television and ordered me to bed. The old Kicks with Coach Flores had been really awesome. They'd moved like a well-oiled machine: pass, pass, score. I already had a ton of ideas about different formations we could try in practice from watching them in action.

The next morning I kept hitting the snooze on my phone alarm. Finally I felt awake enough and grabbed my phone to shut it off. Like always, there was a text waiting for me from Kara. But this morning's was different. No photo. No outfit description. It just said:

Everything ok? U missed our web chat last night!

Oh, no! I had been so wrapped up in the DVD, I had totally forgotten I had promised to web chat with Kara again last night.

Facepalm! ☺ *Totally forgot. Will call tonight and fill u in.*

I felt really bad, and I hoped Kara wasn't too mad at me, but I didn't have time to think about it. I had to hurry up and get dressed so I wouldn't be late for school!

I had so many ideas for practice floating around in my head that I had a hard time concentrating during my classes that day. I kept looking at the clock, and it seemed to tick-tock more and more slowly as the day went on. As soon as school had finished, I headed to the equipment shed. It was over by the field at the school, but the equipment for both the boys' and girls' teams was kept there, so we girls had to drag everything over to the pathetic community field every time we practiced. I thought if I found Coach Flores there early, I could talk to her alone about the thoughts I had.

As I walked across the school field, I noticed someone coming out of the equipment shed. Whoever it was wore a long-sleeved hoodie with the hood pulled up over their head, and long black shorts. *It's a warm day to be wearing a hoodie,* I thought. I was dressed in capris and a T-shirt. I couldn't tell who it was, but I figured it was one of the other Kicks who had come to practice early too.

Then the person walked in the direction of the parking lot, not back toward the field or the locker room.

"Hello?" I called out. But he (or she—I really had no clue!) disappeared out of sight as the sidewalk curved around the parking lot toward the main road.

That's weird, I thought. I looked around nervously. Was anyone else lurking nearby? But there was no one else in sight.

I walked over to the equipment shed and cautiously pulled a door open. It took a second for my eyes to adjust to the darkness inside, because it was so bright out. The shed held balls, flags, paint, nets, and other items. An equipment sign-out sheet hung next to the door with a pen attached by a string.

Nothing looked out of place, until I noticed the Kicks banner lying on the floor. It was usually kept rolled up on a high shelf. Today it sat on the floor and looked a little crumpled.

Suddenly I heard a noise behind me, and the shed grew dark. A figure stood in the doorway, blocking out the sun. I jumped and let out a small scream.

"Who is it?" I yelled, my heart pounding in my chest.

"Devin, what are you doing?" Jessi asked as she stepped inside the shed.

"Thank goodness it's you!" I put a hand to my chest to try to still my heart, which felt like it wanted to leap out of my body. "I saw someone—I'm not sure who—coming out of here. I wanted to check and make sure everything's okay."

"Is it?" Jessi asked curiously.

I shrugged. "It doesn't look like anything is missing, but our banner is definitely out of place." I pointed to it on the floor.

Jessi stooped and picked it up. "Let's bring it outside so we can see better."

We left the darkened shed and stepped out into the bright sun. I held on to one edge of the banner while Jessi pulled the other to unroll it.

We both gasped as we read the banner. It used to say KENTVILLE KICKS, but someone had drawn an arrow between "Kentville" and "Kicks," and at the top of the arrow had written "CAN'T" with a bright red marker. They had also scribbled out the letter S at the end of "Kicks."

"Kentville . . . Can't . . . Kick." Jessi read each word aloud slowly. Then she grew angry. "Kentville can't kick?"

My mouth dropped open. How awful! Who would do such a thing?

"Sabotage! I told you!" she yelled. "Someone is out to get us. And this has Mirabelle written all over it! Do you believe me now?"

I exhaled loudly, still shaken up. "I'm beginning to. There is no explaining this away. It wasn't an accident, or a coincidence, or a mix-up. Someone did this deliberately."

Jessi's eyes grew wide. "We need to look for clues!" She pulled both of the shed doors open wide. "We'll need more light so we can see."

We stepped inside again, our eyes searching all over the shed.

Jessi stepped underneath the shelf where the banner was usually kept. "So someone had to stand right here in order to grab it," she said as she looked around.

"What's this?" she cried as her gaze went to the floor directly under the shelf. Something that looked like a piece of string sat on the ground. I grabbed it and held it in a ray of light that was coming through the door. It was a simple yet colorful two-string friendship bracelet made out of yarn.

"A friendship bracelet," Jessi said thoughtfully. "Lots of kids wear them."

But as I looked at the bracelet in my hand, something seemed familiar about it.

I gasped. "Jessi—the colors! Purple and gold!"

"Those are Pinewood colors!" Jessi practically shouted. "I knew Mirabelle was behind this."

"We've got to tell Coach!" I said.

CHAPTER NINE

For the second time in two days, I made a mad dash into Coach's office. But this time Jessi was with me, and she was carrying the ruined banner.

"Yikes!" Coach Flores cried as we both flew into the room. "That's it! I'm going to have speed bumps installed outside my door to slow you down!"

"Sorry, Coach!" I said, panting once again.

"But this is an emergency!" Jessi exclaimed as she placed the banner on top of Coach Flores's desk and rolled it out. "Look!"

Coach Flores read the banner and shook her head. "That's terrible. Where did you find this?"

"In the equipment shed," I said. "As I was walking over there, I saw someone coming out of the shed, and when I went inside, this was lying on the floor."

"Did you see who it was?" Coach asked.

I shook my head. "I even called out, but they didn't answer me."

"This is just the latest thing someone has done to us!" Jessi cried. "First someone sent a message from a fake e-mail address telling some of the Kicks that practice would start late. Devin's soccer bag got stolen. Then someone claiming to be you called the community center and canceled our practice. At the boys' game a soccer ball exploded. Someone is trying to sabotage the Kangaroos!" Then she paused dramatically before saying, "We know who it is. We even have proof."

She pulled the friendship bracelet out of her pocket and slapped it on top of the banner.

"We found this in the shed, right underneath the shelf where the banner is stored," Jessi continued. "It's a friendship bracelet. A *purple-and-gold* bracelet. Pinewood colors. I'm pretty sure Mirabelle and the Panthers are behind all of this!"

Coach sighed. "First of all, girls, I'm so sorry someone pulled such a mean prank. But honestly, it could have been anybody right here at Kentville. Maybe they thought they were being funny or something. I just find it hard to believe that the Panthers would go to all this trouble. That bracelet could have been dropped the last time the Panthers played Kentville."

"But how would it get into the equipment shed?" Jessi asked.

Coach Flores shrugged. "A strong wind? Or it could

have been stuck to the bottom of someone's cleats. There are a lot of possible explanations."

Jessi shook her head. "Can't you see? Everything is pointing to the Panthers. They want to see us lose."

"Are you sure? None of these"—she paused, searching for the right word—"*events* has negatively impacted the team. Don't forget, you're on a winning streak now!"

Jessi groaned. "That's what Cody said. But the Panthers are messing with us, trying to psych us out. And who knows what they have planned for us next? Maybe something way worse that will actually cause us to lose this time!"

I nodded. "Coach, at first I didn't believe Jessi either. It was easy to explain away all that other stuff as a mix-up or something, but the banner was done deliberately. You can't deny that."

Coach looked thoughtful. "I guess if you add it all together, it is a little suspicious. But a bracelet doesn't prove anything."

"We can't just sit back and do nothing!" Jessi cried.

I nodded my head in agreement. We had to put a stop to this!

Coach sighed again. "The only thing I can suggest right now is to bring your case to the league director, Ms. Carides. She'll listen to what you've just told me, and if she finds enough evidence, she could give the Panthers a warning or even disqualify them for the rest of the season. But it will be up to her."

"Great! When can we go talk to her?" Jessi said.

"I'll call her now and set up an appointment," she said. "Now shake this off and go warm up, girls. We've still got to practice!"

Jessi and I left her office and headed into the locker room to change.

"I can't wait till those Pinewood jerks get what they deserve," Jessi said as we walked in. The rest of the team was suiting up for practice.

"I don't care about revenge," I said. "I just want all this sabotage to stop, if that's what it is."

"You want what to stop?" Grace asked curiously, looking up as she tied her cleats.

"Hey, what's going on?" Emma asked.

The rest of the Kicks huddled around us, wanting to hear the story.

Jessi explained about the banner, and a shocked silence fell over the group.

"That is harsh," Anna said loudly, breaking the silence.

An angry murmur filled the locker room. No surprise, the Kicks weren't happy to hear this news.

"Now put it all together," Jessi said, her hands on her hips. "Remember that fake e-mail from Coach Flores? And how Devin's bag went missing and someone canceled our practice? And did you hear how the boys' soccer ball was tampered with at their game against the Roses? This is not a coincidence. The Panthers are trying to ruin our season!"

"What should we do?" Alandra asked. She sounded panicked.

Jessi explained about our appointment with the league director. A lot of the girls started talking excitedly among themselves, while some of them asked Jessi questions.

I began to worry that maybe we shouldn't have told everybody everything. If whatever was happening was meant to throw us off our game, it would only work if the entire team got paranoid. I wanted the Kicks to focus on practice and winning, not on someone trying to sabotage us!

Practice that day was rough. Instead of focusing, girls would stop and start whispering to each other on the field, clearly still rattled by the news. But Jessi had no problem concentrating. In fact, she seemed thrilled that people were finally starting to believe her.

Friday's practice went a little better, but our rhythm seemed off. It had me worried. If this kept up, we would be exiting the Play-offs Express!

After practice Coach drove Jessi and me to the Gilmore County Middle School Soccer League's office, located at the community center in Adams, a town only a few miles away. She had made the appointment and gotten permission from our parents to take us over.

As we drove into the parking lot, I saw the Atoms, the Adams soccer team, practicing in the field next to the community center. It was just a coincidence that their practice field was next to the league building, but it got me thinking. We hadn't played them yet, but I'd heard they were pretty good. As Jessi and Coach walked into the building, I stopped to watch the Atoms' practice, wondering what drills they were running.

"Uh, Devin?" Jessi said. "Come on!"

"Sorry!" I ran over to catch up. I started to get that butterfly feeling in my stomach again. "League director" sounded so important. What if she didn't believe us? I was starting to wish we hadn't even come.

We were shown into Ms. Carides's office, and she stood up as we entered the room. A tall, thin woman about Coach's age, she had long, dark hair.

"Maria." Ms. Carides smiled warmly at Coach Flores. "It's nice to see you again."

"You too, Beatriz," Coach replied. "I'd like you to meet Jessi and Devin." Ms. Carides smiled at us both. "As I mentioned on the phone yesterday, they have some concerns about possible misconduct from players on one of the other teams."

"Please have a seat," she said, and gestured to the chairs. I sat down nervously, feeling awkward. But Jessi looked confident. It was obvious she couldn't wait to tell Ms. Carides everything.

"Who would like to begin?" Ms. Carides asked, looking between me and Jessi.

"I will!" Jessi jumped in eagerly. She outlined everything that had happened so far and ended with a flourish, placing the friendship bracelet on Ms. Carides's desk. "And here's our proof!"

Ms. Carides picked up the bracelet and held it in her hand, staring at it thoughtfully.

"Girls, there is certainly not enough proof for me to bring any action against the Panthers," she said firmly. "The Kicks may be having a better season this year than last, but let's face it, you got off to a very rocky start this year. I'm not exactly sure if another team would be so threatened by you that they would go to such extremes."

I felt my cheeks blaze red, and saw Jessi frown. Basically she was saying we weren't good enough to be the subject of sabotage!

"But the banner is definite proof that someone is messing with us," Jessi pointed out. "Isn't that at least poor sportsmanship or something?"

"For all we know, that banner might have been defaced by someone from Kentville," Ms. Carides pointed out.

Jessi looked angry. "But the bracelet—"

"Is what would be called circumstantial evidence in any court of law," the league director interrupted. Then she sighed. "You are clearly a team that is finding itself this season, and I do commend all of you and Coach Flores for the hard work you've done. My recommendation is to focus on practice and not worry about these other distractions. Strong practices will continue to strengthen your team." She handed the bracelet back to Jessi.

Coach Flores quickly stood up, looking offended. "Thank you for taking the time to hear the girls out, Beatriz," Coach Flores said crisply. "Girls, please thank Ms. Carides for her time."

"Thanks," I mumbled, looking at the floor. This had

been a disaster. Jessi mumbled something too, but I could barely hear what she said.

Shoulders slumped, we left the office. No one said a word until we were back in the parking lot.

"She thinks we stink!" Jessi cried angrily.

"Now, Jessi," Coach said in a soothing tone of voice. "She suggested you focus on practice and continuing to improve. It's a valid point."

"That's what I've been saying all along!" I said, totally exasperated. That had been so embarrassing! "Ms. Carides is right. We should be worried about practices and improving, not this other stuff."

Jessi glared at me, her arms crossed in front of her. I glared back. Coach sighed. "Oh, dear," she said sadly. "Girls, you've got to let this go. Don't let it get to you. Remember, we're a team!"

We drove back to the school mostly in silence, Jessi and I barely speaking. If someone was really trying to sabotage us, then it was working! The Kicks were starting to come apart.

CHAPTER TEN

"Eye of newt and toe of frog,
Wool of bat and tongue of dog,
Adder's fork and blind-worm's sting,
Lizard's leg and owlet's wing,
For a charm of powerful trouble,
Like a hell-broth boil and bubble."

I watched, wide-eyed, as Frida recited the creepy words over a plastic cauldron in the rehearsal room at the Dramaworks Acting Studio. Her acting class was giving a special performance for family and friends. Frida had on a long, gray robe, and her hair looked messy and hung over her eyes. Even though she didn't have any makeup on her face, she looked incredibly scary, and her voice was so spooky that it gave me chills. Now I understood why she wanted to be an actress. She was amazing!

She and two other girls dressed in gray robes danced around the cauldron. "Double, double toil and trouble; Fire burn and cauldron bubble!" they chanted, and I actually felt a little spooked.

When the scene finished, a woman with sandy-brown hair stepped in front of them.

"That was from *Macbeth*, act 4, scene 1," she said. "Let's give a hand for our students."

The audience clapped as the girls took a bow. Frida's eyes were shining. Next to me Emma let out a cheer.

"Whoo! Go, Frida!"

Emma, Zoe, Jessi, and I had come to see some short Shakespeare scenes that the members of Frida's acting class had prepared. Honestly, I hadn't been sure what to expect, but I'd really liked it. They'd picked a bunch of short, exciting scenes, and even though everyone had been talking like they did hundreds of years ago, it had still been easy to figure out what was going on. The scene with the witches closed the show, so we rushed up to Frida.

"You were awesome!" Emma cried, hugging her.

"Totally scary," Zoe added.

Jessi nodded. "You make an awesome witch."

Frida grinned. "Thanks. I was thinking I could use the character at our next game. Imagine if we could put a spell on the other team so that none of their kicks would reach the goal?"

Jessi giggled. "Or we could turn the Panthers into toads."

"That wouldn't be a fair game," I pointed out. "I just

know that we're both going to make the play-offs, and when we face them there, I want to beat them fair and square."

"But what if *they* don't play fair and square?" Jessi asked, looking right at me.

"Come on. Let's go eat," Frida said, changing the subject. "Acting makes me absolutely ravenous!"

Frida's mom had arranged to take us to Chan's Dragon Inn after the performance, so we all piled into the car and headed out to the restaurant. I'd never been there before; inside, it looked like something out of a movie, with gold dragon statues on pedestals, ruby-red tablecloths, and a big fish tank with orange fish swimming in it by the front door.

"I love this place," Frida said. "It's so glamorous, isn't it?"

"I like how it smells in here," Jessi remarked. "Now *I'm* feeling absolutely ravenous!"

Frida's three aunts walked in behind us, and Frida's mom sat at a table with them and let the five of us Kicks sit at the table next to them. I opened up the big menu and stared at the pages; there must have been a hundred different dishes, but I knew what I wanted.

"Chicken and broccoli, please," I said when the waiter took our order.

Jessi ordered beef lo mein, Emma asked for dumplings, and Zoe ordered the same as I had. And then it was Frida's turn.

"Szechuan tofu please," she said, "and we'll all have

a cup of hot and sour soup. And tea for the table." The waiter gave a little bow and left us.

"Hot and sour soup?" Jessi asked with a grimace.

"Trust me. You'll love it," Frida said. "Anyway, I wanted to thank you guys for coming. It was just an informal preview, but we'll be doing a full show in a couple of months, and that should be amazing."

"You are totally the best one in the class," I told her.

Frida blushed a little. "Thanks," she replied. "It's a really cool role to play. The witches are the ones who set the whole play into motion. They're the ones who tell Macbeth that he's destined to be king, and then he takes destiny into his own hands and kills the king so he can take his place."

Emma shuddered. "That's horrible!"

Jessi gave me another look. "Yes, people are capable of awful things. Like sabotage!"

I sighed. "Can't we just forget about it?"

"Are you talking about the banner?" Emma asked. "I still can't believe that someone would do that to us."

"It's not just someone; it's the Panthers," Jessi said firmly.

"Maybe it's just Mirabelle," Frida added thoughtfully. "In Macbeth it's his wife, Lady Macbeth, who's really behind everything. Maybe Mirabelle is like the Lady Macbeth of the Panthers."

"I'm not sure about the Macbeth stuff, but I think you're right about Mirabelle," Jessi agreed, leaning forward. "After all, she's the only one with a really personal connection to the Kicks."

Zoe nodded. "You're right. It's got to really bug her that she transferred to the Panthers and thought she was going to be so much better than us, but we beat them."

"And we already know that Mirabelle was at the game when Devin's uniform was stolen," Jessi pointed out. "She is the most obvious suspect."

"Listen, I'll admit that this kind of makes sense," I said. "But what are we supposed to do? We already talked to Ms. Carides about it, and she told us to focus and practice. I agree with her."

"Who's Ms. Carides?" Emma asked.

"She's the league director," I replied. "Coach Flores took us to talk to her, and we explained everything, but she didn't really believe us."

"Even after I showed her the evidence." Jessi took the friendship bracelet out of her pocket. "Panthers colors. I found it in the equipment room."

Emma, Zoe, and Frida looked shocked.

"No way!" Emma cried. "How could she not believe you after seeing this?"

Zoe shook her head. "That's so not fair."

"Exactly," I said. "But there's nothing we can do except keep our eyes open and play our best."

Jessi got a devious look on her face. "Unless we get more proof."

"And how do we do that?" I asked.

"I could spy on Mirabelle," Jessi replied.

"That sounds ridiculous," I said. "What do you mean, 'spy'?"

"Like, follow her around and see what she does," Jessi answered. "Didn't you ever read *Harriet the Spy*? She got the dirt on everybody."

"That is an amazing idea," Frida said. "Do you want me to go undercover?"

"No, I got this," Jessi replied. "Mirabelle and I used to be besties, remember? I know where she hangs out. We don't have a game tomorrow, so I can follow her around."

Zoe shuddered. "You mean, like, stalk her? That sounds super creepy."

"Harriet the Spy wasn't creepy. She was cute," Jessi pointed out.

"Well, you'd just be, like, keeping an eye on things, right?" Emma asked Jessi. "Maybe that's not so bad. If you do find something out, it could help us."

Jessi nodded. "Exactly. So far, Mirabelle's been trying to psych us out. Devin, you keep saying that you want us to get to the play-offs. Well, what if she messes that up for us? She deserves to be spied on."

I just shook my head. "This whole thing is crazy."

Then the waiter came back and put a small, steaming bowl of soup in front of each of us.

"Thank goodness! I was about to faint!" Frida cried, picking up her spoon.

The soup was a weird orangey color, and it looked like

it had papery things floating in it, but I put my spoon in and took a taste. It was yummy—hot and spicy and definitely a little sour, which kind of matched my mood.

I wasn't going to stop Jessi from spying on Mirabelle—and I knew that I couldn't, even if I wanted to. I really hoped that Jessi wouldn't find out anything, and that all the sabotage or whatever would just stop, but I had a feeling that things were going to get worse before they got better.

I had no idea just how right I'd be.

CHAPTER ELEVEN

"Good news, guys," Zoe announced at lunch on Monday. She held up her right wrist. "The sling is off. But I still have to wear the bandage."

"Does this mean you can play?" I asked.

Zoe crossed her fingers. "Still waiting to be cleared."

"That's so great!" Emma said. She turned to Jessi. "So, what happened with . . . you know?"

Jessi looked around, like she was making sure nobody was listening.

"Okay, let me give you guys a report," she said in a hushed voice. "So, Mirabelle is a total mall rat. She always has been. I checked the Panthers' practice schedule and saw they had a practice at noon yesterday, so I asked my dad to drop me off at the mall at two o'clock. I hung out in front of Crush, her favorite store. I was there for, like, a half hour, and she didn't show up. But then there she was. I had her right in my sights." She smiled triumphantly.

"Wait. How come she didn't see you?" Emma asked.

"Because I wore a disguise." Jessi held out her phone and showed us a photo she had snapped of herself. She wore giant sunglasses and had tucked her braids into a blue baseball cap. She also had on some kind of beige trench coat with the collar stuck up, and I figured she must have borrowed it from her mom.

Emma giggled. "Oh my gosh. You look like something out of a spy movie."

"I looked inconspicuous," Jessi replied seriously. "She never saw me."

"So you just stood there like a stalker and watched her shop?" Zoe asked.

"No, I pretended I was reading a magazine," Jessi replied. "And it worked. Anyway, she was there with a bunch of the Panthers. They looked at clothes for a while, and then they moved on to the food court, so I followed them."

Frida leaned across the table, hanging on Jessi's every word. "Did you hear them plotting their next move against us?"

Jessi shook her head. "No. I sat two tables away, and I could pretty much hear everything they said, and they were mostly talking about boys and their next game."

"See? There's nothing more to worry about," I said.

"But I'm not done yet," Jessi said with a gleam in her eye. "I got some very important evidence."

She held out her phone again and showed us a picture of an arm.

"I don't get it," I said.

"This is Mirabelle's arm," Jessi informed us. "And what's key in the picture is what's *not* in it. Namely, Mirabelle's friendship bracelet."

"What do you mean?" Emma asked.

"I mean, Mirabelle was not wearing her bracelet, but all of the other Panthers were," Jessi answered, her voice rising with excitement. "Don't you see? Mirabelle's bracelet is the one we found in the equipment shed. Mirabelle is the one who's been sabotaging us!"

Frida gasped, and Emma and Zoe looked surprised.

"You may be right," I admitted. "So if it's just Mirabelle, then we can confront her, right?"

Jessi grinned. "Yeah, you can count me in on that."

"I think we should talk to Coach Flores before we do anything," Emma suggested.

"We tried that already," Jessi reminded her. "And all that happened was that we ended up getting insulted by the league director."

"But this is more evidence," I pointed out. "It couldn't hurt."

Jessi sighed. "Fine. But if it doesn't do any good, then I vote for confronting Mirabelle."

When we got to the locker room that afternoon, Coach Flores was waiting by the door—and she was holding my duffel bag!

"You found it!" I cried. "But how?"

"It's kind of a strange story," Coach replied as the other Kicks gathered around us to hear. "Mr. Jenkins, one of the maintenance workers, dropped it off to me this morning. He was working here yesterday, and he said somebody ran up to the door by the gym, put it down, and left."

"Did he see who it was?" I asked.

Coach shook her head. "He said it was a girl with blond hair. He called out to her, but she didn't answer."

I unzipped the bag. "I hope everything's still here."

I pulled out my shorts, the pink SportsWrap for my headband, and then my jersey. It unrolled as I took it out, and to my shock I saw the word "Loser" scrawled across the front in some kind of black marker. A big stain of purple dye streaked across the bottom.

I stared at the shirt, unable to speak, but I could hear the other Kicks gasp. Everyone started talking at once.

"No way!"

"That's awful!"

"Oh my gosh!"

"This is too much," Jessi said loudly. "Remember when Mirabelle called us losers? She's really rubbing it in. And that Panthers purple is just another insult."

"But didn't the janitor say that the girl who dropped it off had blond hair?" Emma asked.

Coach Flores nodded. "Yes, he did. So if you are saying that Mirabelle did this, that would rule her out."

"Unless she wore a wig," Frida suggested.

Then I thought of something. "Coach, did Mr. Jenkins say what time he saw the girl drop it off?"

Coach thought. "I think he said it was around three o'clock."

I looked right at Jessi. "Then it couldn't have been Mirabelle," I said. I wanted to say, *Because you were spying on her*, but I didn't want Coach Flores to know that.

Jessi nodded. "So it was another one of the Panthers, then. They must be working on this together after all."

Coach Flores sighed. "Girls, I am sorry this is happening to you. It's very poor sportsmanship. I'll contact Ms. Carides about this right away."

"Don't bother," Jessi said. "She totally insulted us. We don't need her help. And she'd probably just tell us to practice more or something anyway."

Coach Flores looked sad. "You might be right, Jessi, I'm sorry to say. But I can still try to talk to her. She may change her mind."

I looked around, and pretty much the whole team was there, and they all looked upset. The Panthers' sabotage was working, and as co-captain I couldn't let it bring down the team.

"It's just a dumb jersey," I said loudly. "Forget about it. We need a good practice today so we can beat the Atoms this weekend."

Grace spoke up. "That's right. We can't let whoever's doing this psych us out. So let's get ready!"

"That's the right attitude," Coach Flores said with a smile. "I'm proud of you girls."

We all headed to the benches to get changed, and even though I had just told the team to concentrate on practice, I couldn't. I was boiling mad. I crumpled up the jersey and stuffed it in the bottom of the duffel bag.

Jessi walked up to me. "You know, I was thinking it's time to send the Panthers a message."

"Forget it," I said. "We can't start getting distracted by this stuff. That's just what the Panthers want."

"But we can't let them get away with it!" Jessi protested.

"We'll talk later," I said as I knotted the SportsWrap before sliding it onto my head. "Let's get through practice first, okay?"

Jessi frowned. "It's like you're not even listening, Devin," she said, and then she stomped off.

CHAPTER TWELVE

I definitely did not like arguing with Jessi.

Mirabelle would love it if she knew we were fighting, I thought. *This is just what she wants.*

There was no point in talking to Jessi during practice. She ignored me for most of it, anyway. I thought I could talk to her when we were waiting for our rides home, but something else happened. As we walked away from the field, I saw Steven over by the parking lot. He waved and ran up to me.

"Hey, Devin, can I talk to you?"

"Um, sure," I replied, glancing over at Jessi. But she had already walked past without looking at me.

"So, uh, how was practice?" Steven asked.

"Good," I said. Why was it that whenever I was around him, I couldn't seem to talk? "How was yours?"

"Good." He looked down and kicked the grass with his

sneaker. I couldn't help thinking that his spiky hair looked supercute today. He must have added extra gel or something.

He looked up again, and that's when I noticed that his eyes were that gray-green color that you don't see that often. "So, Cody said he asked Jessi to the carnival, and I thought, like, maybe the four of us could go together?"

"You want me to go to the carnival with you?" My voice sounded like I had just swallowed a mouse or something.

Steven nodded. "Yeah, if you want to."

My heart was pounding faster than if I had been winging down the field toward the opposing goal. Part of me was thrilled, and the rest of me was freaked out and confused. Then I remembered my pledge to myself to stay focused on soccer until the season was over.

"Well, yeah, I want to. But we're, like, trying to make the play-offs and everything, and I'm, like, trying to be focused and everything, so . . ." Had I forgotten how to speak English? "I should stay focused on the play-offs for now. But thanks. It's really nice of you."

Steven looked absolutely crushed, and I felt terrible. I immediately thought about changing my answer, but he didn't give me a chance.

"Okay. Well, then, see you around," he said, and then he raced off like he was being chased or something.

I still felt terrible, and more confused than before. I mean, I liked Steven, I really did, and part of me kind of liked the idea of going to the carnival with him and Jessi and Cody. But part of me was supernervous about it.

The honk of a horn got me out of my thoughts, and I saw Mom's car at the edge of the parking lot. I quickly ran to it and hopped into the front seat.

"Who was that you were talking to?" Mom asked.

"Oh, that's just Steven," I answered, looking out the window. "He's on the boys' team."

"Devin has a boyfriend! Devin has a boyfriend!" Maisie chanted from the backseat.

I turned around to look at her. "He is *not* my boyfriend."

Maisie made a face. "Good! Boys are gross! Ew!"

"What about Riley? Didn't you just have a playdate with him?" I asked.

"Riley doesn't count," Maisie protested. "He's nice."

"Well, so is Steven," I said. Satisfied, I turned back around.

That night I told Kara about what had happened.

"I mean, I like him, but I need to stay focused on soccer right now," I said.

"Or are you just using that as an excuse?" Kara asked.

I thought about that. I definitely was kind of afraid of going out on an actual date, and the soccer excuse certainly was convenient.

"Maybe," I said, and sighed. "I guess it doesn't matter now. He'll probably never ask me out again."

"If he really likes you, he will," Kara said.

"Thanks."

Then I got a message on the screen that Jessi was trying to connect with me.

"Hey, that's Jessi. Mind if I get it?" I asked.

"All right," Kara said, but her voice was flat. "See you tomorrow."

"It's just that—" I wanted to explain to Kara about the fight, and how I needed to make things right with Jessi, but she logged off before I could finish.

Jessi's face appeared on the screen next.

"Are you still mad at me?" I blurted out.

"Well, kind of," she admitted. "Listen, I didn't mean to storm off like that. It's just . . . I'm frustrated. We need to do something. We can't just sit around and let Mirabelle get to us."

"We should just ignore it," I said.

"And wait till she does something worse?" Jessi asked. "No way."

I sighed. "Jessi, I don't want to fight, okay? I just don't agree with you."

"I don't want to fight either," Jessi replied. "Just promise me something. I have an idea. I'll tell everybody at lunch. Just promise me you'll listen, okay?"

I didn't want to fight with Jessi anymore. "Okay. I'll listen."

"You're gonna love this. Just wait," Jessi said, her brown eyes gleaming. "Bye!"

The screen went dark. Once again it seemed Jessi was getting to be just as dramatic as Frida! But I had to admit, I was curious to know what she had in mind.

The next day Jessi asked me, Emma, Zoe, and Frida to meet outside in the library courtyard for lunch.

"So here's the plan," she announced once we all got there. "I spent some time scrolling through the Panthers' group profile page online, and they're always complaining about how their coach is a sunscreen freak."

"Well, sunscreen is very important," Emma said.

"That's beside the point," Jessi said quickly. "So the Panthers have a ten o'clock practice on Sunday. If we get to their field early, we can add this to their sunscreen bottles."

She held up a small bottle. I leaned close to read the label.

"Blue food coloring?" I asked.

"Perfectly safe and harmless, but it will get our point across," Jessi said. "They use spray sunscreen, so they won't see the blue until it's on their skin. Then they'll be Kicks blue. It'll be classic."

Zoe looked horrified. "But that's terrible! And won't we get in big trouble?"

"How?" Jessi asked. "They won't be able to prove it's us, just like we can't prove that they sabotaged our banner."

"I don't know," Zoe said nervously. "I just got the sling off. I don't want to do anything risky."

"I'll do it!" Frida said eagerly. "But how will we get there?"

"I've already got it worked out," Jessi informed us. "The Panthers field is next to Pinewood Park, which has this really cool outdoor training course. I told my mom that we wanted to do the course Sunday morning to get ready for our game, and she already said she'd take us."

I shook my head. "No way, Jessi. I've listened long enough. This plan is insane."

"It is not," Jessi protested. "The Panthers' pranks are getting bigger and bigger. What if their next prank makes us lose a game?"

Then we might not get into the play-offs, I admitted to myself. Jessi definitely had me intrigued.

"So this way we send a message," Jessi said. "A message that they can't mess around with us anymore. It's for our own protection."

"A message doesn't sound so drastic," Emma said timidly.

"It's a great idea!" Frida agreed. "If we don't do something now, who knows what will happen?"

My friends were starting to make sense. Or maybe I was just afraid of what the Panthers might do next. We had been playing so well, and I didn't want to lose just because of some stupid stunts the Panthers were playing. I looked at my friends.

"So you all agree with Jessi?" I asked.

"Definitely!" Frida said, and Emma nodded. Zoe looked at me.

"I guess, if you do, Devin," she said hesitantly.

I took a deep breath. "The blue stuff washes off, right?" Jessi nodded. "Easily."

"Then maybe it's not a bad idea," I said. "We should tell

Grace, though. After all, she's co-captain and this involves the whole team."

"No!" Jessi hissed. "I mean, we need to keep this small. And that way, if something goes wrong, the rest of the team is cleared."

"What do you mean, 'if something goes wrong'?" Zoe asked nervously.

"Nothing will go wrong," Jessi said quickly. "But you have to be prepared for anything. So are you with me?"

"Yes!" Frida and Emma cheered.

Zoe nodded. "I guess. As long as you're sure we won't get caught."

"We won't," Jessi said firmly.

I didn't answer right away. Jessi had a good point about not telling Grace. A million things could go wrong if the whole team got involved. But if we kept it simple . . .

"I'm in," I said finally, and Jessi let out a whoop.

"Let's get ready for some revenge!"

CHAPTER THIRTEEN

"Good morning, Devin!" Mrs. Dukes said cheerfully as I climbed into Jessi's minivan Sunday morning. Zoe and Frida sat in the very back while I took the seat next to Emma. Jessi turned around from the front passenger seat to grin at me.

"I have to say, I'm impressed with you girls and your dedication," Mrs. Dukes said. "A training course in the morning, and a game this afternoon!"

Zoe made a little grimace, and I felt the same way. We weren't exactly being truthful about why we wanted to go to Pinewood Park, and I felt guilty about that.

Luckily, Mrs. Dukes kept right on talking, saving us from having to answer.

"You all have motivated me to get back into my fitness routine," she said. "While you girls are doing the training course, I'll be walking. I've got my iPod all ready to go, thanks to Jessi."

Jessi smiled. "I've got some surprises for you on there, Mom."

"Uh-oh," Mrs. Dukes groaned, while the rest of us laughed.

She pulled up to the park, which was pretty empty, since it was only eight thirty on a Sunday morning, even though it was another beautiful, sunny day.

We all piled out of the van, and Mrs. Dukes, wearing a turquoise-and-black tracksuit, started doing some stretches.

"Will an hour be enough time to do the course?" Mrs. Dukes asked as she did a leg lunge.

Jessi nodded. "That should be plenty of time, Mom. Thanks!"

Pinewood Park was very pretty, I thought as I looked around. And pretty fancy, too, but I had kind of expected that since it was so close to Pinewood, the private middle school that Mirabelle now went to. We had parked in the lot closest to the children's playground, and in the distance I could see tennis courts and a field with a picnic area. Everything was superclean and nicely landscaped, with green trees and shrubbery everywhere you looked.

Where we stood, the walking path went to the right or the left. The stops for the fitness trail were placed around the walking path.

Jessi nudged me and whispered into my ear, "We need to go to the left. That's the quickest way to the Panthers' field."

Mrs. Dukes stopped stretching and popped an earbud into her ear.

"I'm off!" she said happily. "We'll meet back here in an hour, then."

She started walking on the path to the right, and we stopped at the first stop on the fitness trail on the left. It was a bar to do pull-ups on. I hated doing pull-ups, but I reached up and pulled myself up. Emma, Jessi, and Frida did the same, until Mrs. Dukes was out of sight.

Zoe shook her head. "I don't think pull-ups are a good idea for my wrist just yet. But I've got some bad news. The doctor wants me to wait one more week before playing again."

I felt bad for the team, but I felt worse for Zoe. I knew I'd be going crazy if I couldn't play for three weeks.

"That's okay," I said. "I'm just glad you're getting better."

Jessi dropped down from the pull-up bar and looked around.

"Come on. Let's go," she said.

We followed behind her, and Zoe kept looking around.

"You're sure nobody's going to catch us, right?" she asked nervously.

"Yeah," Jessi replied. "Well, mostly sure."

Zoe turned pale, and I definitely sympathized. I felt the butterflies begin a jamboree in my own stomach, especially when the path curved and I could see the Panthers' field. It had been the scene of our biggest defeat and our greatest win this season. And now it would be the place where we finally got even for all the mean tricks Mirabelle and the Panthers had been playing on us!

Since Pinewood was an exclusive, expensive school, the grounds and buildings were really impressive. The gym and locker rooms were housed in their own shiny new building, flanking the field. We left the walking path and crossed over until we were behind the gym. A couple of cars sat in the parking lot. Since the Panthers didn't have practice until ten a.m., none of the players were here yet. At least we hoped.

"The coach might be inside," Jessi whispered as we all crouched in some bushes, watching the building. "But that's a good thing. It will mean the door will be open."

"Wait." I put out a hand to stop Jessi as she started to leave our hiding place in the bushes. "If the Panthers aren't here yet, the sunscreen won't be here either."

Jessi smiled. "Yes, it will. I checked the Panthers' online profile again, and the coach posted a whole flyer about it. She stores it in the locker room so there are no excuses, and if players don't use, it, they can't play. She's, like, a serious sunscreen freak.

"If we get caught inside the locker room," Jessi continued, "we'll just say we were looking for the bathroom. Okay?"

Zoe's eyes got really wide and the color left her face. "Ugh. I think I'm going to be sick."

"We'll be fine, Zoe. Don't worry!" Emma said, patting Zoe's shoulder.

Frida grinned at Jessi. "I think this is totally fun!" she said, and Jessi grinned back.

Zoe and I exchanged glances. I guess we were the only nervous ones in the group. I gulped.

"Remember 'Kentville Can't Kick' and 'Loser,'" Jessi reminded me, trying to rile me up for revenge.

Mirabelle's laughing, gloating face popped into my mind, to be quickly replaced by her turned Smurf blue. She totally had it coming! Jessi's tactic had worked.

"Let's do this!" I said.

"The girls' locker room is this way." Jessi pointed to a side door with GIRLS written on the front. We walked over to it, and Jessi pulled on the handle. The door swung open.

"We're in," Jessi whispered with a smile.

We crept into the hall and turned left. When we heard music playing, we stopped in our tracks. A light was on, coming from the office directly in front of the girls' locker room.

"The coach!" Zoe whispered loudly, her eyes wide with fear.

Jessi put a finger to her lips and crept closer to the door. She peered inside quickly before lowering her head and coming back to us.

"The coach is in there. She's got the radio on," Jessi said. "But luckily the door is shut. The top part is glass, but the bottom is solid. If we crawl past the door, she won't see us."

Jessi dropped to her knees and started to shuffle forward. Frida and Emma quickly followed her. I looked at

Zoe, and I knew we were both feeling the same. What if the coach looked out the window? Or opened the door? We'd be toast!

Jessi, Frida, and Emma were past the door already. I had to decide. Turn back, or join my teammates.

Jessi turned and frantically waved for me and Zoe to follow. Emma started to giggle nervously and had to put her hand over her mouth.

"I'm doing it," I whispered to Zoe, and then I crawled forward, practically closing my eyes the whole time. My heart was pounding so loudly, I was sure the Panthers' coach could hear it.

I finally reached the locker room door, and I could hear Zoe behind me. Jessi popped up and opened the door to the locker room. We all quickly scrambled inside.

"I feel like a burglar," I said, flattening myself against the wall. It was a total relief to be out of that hallway, though.

"Phase one, successful," Frida said, and I guessed she was pretending to be some kind of secret agent.

Jessi flicked a switch, illuminating the dark room. *Wow*, I thought, Pinewood sure was a fancy school. Instead of metal lockers there were open wooden shelves. Each one was labeled with the player's name, with a shelf on top that held their shin guards and cleats, and an open closet where their game-day jerseys hung, looking as if they had been professionally cleaned. Underneath were drawers for more storage space.

Jessi started flinging open the drawers and searching.

"No sunscreen!" she cried.

"That's because it's over here," Frida said. There was a large table at the other end of the room. There were cases of water on top, and bottles of sunscreen. A big sign was taped to the wall over the bottles. BURN IT UP ON THE FIELD, NOT ON YOUR SKIN! it read.

Jessi reached inside her pocket and pulled out five little bottles of blue food coloring.

"Here you go!" She handed each one of us a bottle and opened the lid of one of the sunscreen bottles. She poured in some food coloring, closed the bottle, and began to shake.

"Hmmmm." She frowned as she opened up her bottle to peer inside. "We might need to add some water to get it to mix better."

She scanned the locker room. "Let's try this way," Jessi whispered, nodding toward a short hallway. We each carried a bottle of sunscreen and followed her. Doors led to other changing rooms, but luckily we found the bathroom at the very end. Frida had reached to turn on the sink, when we all heard the sound of a door opening.

"Hello? Is someone in here?" a voice called.

Zoe started shaking, the sunscreen bottle trembling in her hand. My own heart began to race. We all looked at one another, eyes wide. Frida turned her head and pointed to a door at the far end of the bathroom, in the opposite direction from where we had just been.

We heard footsteps coming closer and a voice saying, "I could have sworn I turned the lights off."

Jessi jerked her head in the direction of the door Frida had pointed to. We all moved as quickly and quietly as we could through the bathroom and out the door to the other side.

We stepped into a hallway directly in front of the Pinewood gym. The main entrance was only a few steps away. We all raced out the door, through the parking lot, and back to the safety of the bushes bordering Pinewood Park.

"That was close!" Jessi said, breathing hard.

I groaned. "But now we're not pranksters; we're thieves!" I held up the bottle of sunscreen. The other girls still held their bottles too. "We forgot to leave the sunscreen in the locker room."

"We're not thieves if we didn't mean to take the bottles," Jessi argued. "It was an accident."

"Darn!" Frida groaned. "I so wanted to see Mirabelle turned blue!"

"I'm just glad this is over," a relieved Zoe said. "And that we didn't get into any trouble. I'm not cut out for this revenge stuff."

"I don't think I am either, actually," Emma admitted. "I mean, it sounded like fun, but it was mostly terrifying."

Jessi shook her head. "You guys are such chickens. I'm just sorry we didn't get to finish."

"It was exhilarating," Frida said. "Like being onstage."

"If that's what being onstage is like, then I'll never join drama club," I said. My hands were still shaking, I was so nervous. "That was a stupid thing to do."

Almost getting caught made me realize what a big mistake this all had been. We could have all gotten suspended from the team, and then the whole team would have suffered. What kind of co-captain was I? I was supposed to be leading my team into victory, not into trouble.

"Let's get back to the trail," I said firmly. "We need to focus on our game against the Atoms."

"Maybe we could put the sunscreen where they might find it," Emma suggested.

"Let's just leave them on the edge of the parking lot," Jessi said. "I don't think we should go back there."

Nobody argued with her. We put down the sunscreen and then we went back to the fitness trail. We actually ended up completing it just as Mrs. Dukes got back to the start of the trail, fresh from her walk.

"I should get you girls back to Kentville so you have time to eat lunch before your game this afternoon," she said, looking at her watch. "How was the fitness trail?"

We all looked at one another.

"Um, invigorating," Jessi replied.

"You can say that again," Emma said, and Jessi nudged her with her elbow.

After our locker room scare and the fitness trail, we were all pretty worn out as we made our way to the minivan.

"Let's forget this ever happened," I said, and Jessi nodded.

"Emma! Look out!" I cried, but it was too late. The ball soared inches above her head, but a distracted Emma didn't react in time. The Atoms were ahead, 4–1.

The Kicks were struggling on the Atoms' home field. The Atoms' attacks seemed to gain more strength as the game went on, and Emma, still shaken up by the events in the Panthers' locker room this morning, was not at her best. The Atoms defenders were also playing well, putting pressure on the Kicks defense. I'd gotten in a long shot that should have been a goal, but the Atoms goalie made a spectacular save.

The Atoms were clearly having their best game of the season. Too bad it had to be against the Kicks!

Coach pulled Emma out and put in Zarine instead. She successfully blocked an unexpected yet well-placed shot from an Atoms striker. Things seemed to be looking up for the Kicks when Olivia and Grace started several offensive sequences with good clearing passes, but the Atoms were there to block us at every turn.

In the end the Kicks just couldn't catch up. Our winning streak was over. We had lost.

I hung my head and placed my hands on my hips. Letting out a deep sigh, I began to calculate our chances for the play-offs. We still had a shot, even with this loss. But it meant we would have to beat the Rams at our game next Saturday. If we didn't, the Kicks' chance at the trophy would be dashed.

"Great game, ladies!" Coach called to us. "The Atoms really made you hustle. You played terrifically, but they played better today. Sometimes that's just the way it goes. Don't let it get you down."

After saying good-bye to the other Kicks, Jessi and I grabbed our bags and walked off the Atoms' field together. We made our way to the parking lot to meet our parents.

"This stinks," Jessi said. "First our attempt to get back at the Panthers fails, and then we lose."

"Well, maybe we could have played better, but the whole thing this morning—it never should have happened," I said. "I let my emotions get to me, and I should have kept us from making that mistake."

Jessi and I were walking along, both feeling down, when we heard someone call our names. We whirled around, and standing there was Mirabelle!

"I saw you coming out of our locker room," she said with a smug grin. "And I know what you were doing!"

CHAPTER FOURTEEN

"Excuse me?" Jessi asked, her hands on her hips. "You have the nerve to come here and accuse us after everything you and the Panthers have done to the Kicks?"

"What?" Mirabelle asked. She sounded confused. "You're the ones who snuck into our locker room, and why? To steal our sunscreen? What kind of weird prank is that?"

I turned red. So Mirabelle did know about the sunscreen. I wondered what my parents would do when they found out. Probably ground me for a zillion years.

"Oh, really?" Jessi said in disbelief. "So sending out a fake e-mail, stealing Devin's soccer bag, calling the community center to give away our field during practice, tampering with the boys' soccer ball, trashing our banner, and writing 'Loser' on Devin's jersey? That's what you call not having done anything?" Jessi was practically screaming.

Mirabelle looked genuinely shocked. "Somebody did all that to you guys?" Then her expression got angry again. "Wait, and you thought *I* did all that?"

"Of course we did," Jessi shot back. "You know you hate the Kicks."

"I do not hate the Kicks!" Mirabelle protested.

"Um, you did write 'Bye, Losers' on the mirror when you left," I reminded her. "And laughed pretty hard when the boys' team made fun of us at the dance."

Mirabelle bit her lip when I said that, and then she looked away.

"Whatever," she said, but she sounded hurt. "I just can't believe that you'd really think I'd do all that stuff, Jessi."

"Well, I did," Jessi replied.

Mirabelle looked at me. "You too, Devin?"

"Well, yeah," I said slowly. "You and the other girls on the Pinewood team. Somebody stained my jersey Pinewood purple. And we even found a Pinewood bracelet right where our trashed banner was."

"Right!" Jessi said triumphantly. She reached into her bag and pulled out the purple-and-gold friendship bracelet. "Here it is."

"My bracelet!" she sounded shocked. "I haven't seen it since I gave it to Jamie."

"Jamie from the Rams?" I asked.

"Right," Mirabelle replied. "We became friends after being on the travel team together. Jamie is the one who suggested we check you guys out, at that game against the Eagles."

"I saw you two in the stands that day," Jessi remembered.

"Jamie said we should go, since you were doing so much better," Mirabelle said. "You know, to size up our competition. That's when Jamie asked if I wanted to exchange friendship bracelets. I gave her my Pinewood one, and she gave me hers. It's red and yellow for the Rams."

"Why aren't you wearing it, then?" Jessi asked, her arms crossed in front of her.

"I felt weird wearing the Riverdale colors," Mirabelle admitted. "It felt disloyal to the Panthers. So I took it off. I haven't been wearing any bracelet since then. Can I have my bracelet back?"

Jessi looked reluctant to hand it over, and I didn't blame her. It was our only real evidence linking the Panthers to the sabotage.

"First answer me this. Why did you come all the way out to Adams today?" Jessi asked.

"I came early to practice this morning," Mirabelle replied. "I saw you, Devin, Emma, Zoe, and Frida run out of the gym. Then later our coach was freaking out because a bunch of our sunscreen bottles were missing."

"Did you tell your coach that you saw us there?" I asked, my heart beating fast.

Mirabelle shook her head. "I wanted to talk to you first, and I knew you had a game against the Atoms today," she answered. "I guess . . . I might want to beat you on the field, but I didn't want you to get in trouble, Jessi."

Jessi looked surprised. "You didn't?"

Mirabelle shrugged. "I don't know. The girls at Pinewood are really stuck-up. The team is supercompetitive. I guess I kind of miss Kentville . . . and you too, sometimes."

Jessi looked like she was trying to decide whether Mirabelle was messing with her or not. I certainly had never seen Mirabelle be this sincere before.

"Thanks for having my back," Jessi said.

Watching the two of them made me think of me and Kara. We'd been friends for as long as I could remember. Even if we stopped being friends, I knew she would always have a special place in my heart. I guess maybe Mirabelle felt that way too.

Jessi handed her back the bracelet. "I believe you. Sorry we tried to . . . steal your sunscreen."

She gave me a look that warned me not to say anything about the real plan. I don't think she trusted Mirabelle just yet, and I didn't blame her.

Mirabelle shook her head. "That is, like, really lame revenge. But I guess it got our coach mad."

"You guys playing the Vipers this afternoon?" I asked Mirabelle.

She nodded.

"Well, good luck," I said, and I meant it.

"Thanks," Mirabelle said. "Later."

"That was weird," I said, shaking my head.

"That was more like the old Mirabelle, the one who used to be my friend," Jessi said a little wistfully. "At least she's not going to tell anyone about the sunscreen."

"Do you believe her? About not telling, and the sabotage stuff?" I asked.

"Yeah," Jessi replied, "but I'm not so sure about the sabotage stuff. Although, she really didn't seem to have any idea what we were talking about."

"Hmmmm," I said slowly as I let everything Mirabelle had told us sink in. "She said she gave her bracelet to Jamie. What if Jamie is the one who wrecked our banner?"

"Mr. Jenkins said the girl who returned your bag had blond hair," Jessi said excitedly. "Jamie has blond hair!"

"And she was at the Eagles game the day my bag was stolen!" I cried. It was all starting to make sense. "Steven said that the Rams were the boys' strongest competition this season, not the Panthers. And the Kicks will face the Rams in a week."

Jessi snapped her fingers. "Jamie could have even planted Mirabelle's bracelet in the shed to throw us off her trail!"

"Wow, pretty diabolical for a middle school student." I shook my head in disbelief. "So if the Rams are behind this—"

Jessi finished my sentence. "Then we targeted the wrong team!"

CHAPTER FIFTEEN

We made our way to the parking lot, still stunned by what we had learned. My dad, mom, and sister were waiting by our car, talking with Jessi's parents. Emma, Frida, and Zoe were huddled off to the side, clearly comforting Emma, who'd had a not-so-great game.

"You okay, kiddo?" My dad asked, ruffling my hair with his hand.

I readjusted my pink headband and gave him a sad smile. "It would have been worse if this loss had ended our shot at the play-offs, but we've still got another chance at our game against the Rams next week."

Jessi gave me a look, her eyebrows raised. It was easy to tell what she was thinking. We had a shot if the Rams didn't try to sabotage us again!

"That's my girl! I love that positive attitude," Dad said with a grin. "But I figured you still might need a little cheering up. That's why we're going to take you all out for ice cream. Mr. and Mrs. Dukes are coming with us, and we got the okay from Frida's, Zoe's, and Emma's parents to take them, too."

Jessi and I exchanged excited glances. We couldn't wait to tell our friends what we had just discovered!

"I want to sit with Devin and her friends!" Maisie whined as the Kicks all sat in a booth together on the other side of the room from where our parents were going to sit.

"Mom, please?" I begged. "We need to talk soccer strategy."

"Maisie, let Devin have some alone time with her friends," Mom told her.

"Fine." Maisie crossed her arms. "But I'm getting two scoops, then!"

My mom dragged a complaining Maisie away while Jessi laughed. "We should send Maisie after the Rams. That will stop them!"

Emma, Zoe, and Frida looked confused. "After the Rams? What are you talking about?" Frida wondered.

I cleared my throat. "Wait until you hear this!" Jessi and I filled them in about our conversation with Mirabelle and how we'd figured out it was the Rams, not the Panthers, sabotaging us.

"So Lady Macbeth is Jamie Quinn, not Mirabelle!" Frida said.

Emma shook her head. "I can't believe it. The Rams? What have they got against us?"

"Well, I can't believe that Mirabelle was actually nice," Zoe said. "She really promised not to say anything about the sunscreen?"

I nodded. "I think she meant it," I replied, and Zoe looked relieved.

"The Rams," Frida repeated thoughtfully. "Hmm. The plot thickens."

"But wait!" Zoe cried. She sat up straight in her chair, holding her ice cream spoon in the air. "We're playing the Rams next week!"

"Forget about trying to get any kind of revenge on them," I said firmly. "If we play well, we'll win. We can beat them fair and square."

Zoe shook her head. "That's not what I meant. We're playing the Rams next Saturday, and so are the boys! Both home games on the same day. If the Rams are planning any more sabotage, that's gotta be when they'll try it."

Emma's eyes grew wide. "How can we stop them? We don't even know what they have planned."

Frida had an idea. "What if you bring it to the league director again? What was her name?"

"Ms. Carides," I said. "That's not a bad idea. We have actual evidence this time."

"Not really," Jessi objected. "All we have is Mirabelle's word that she gave Jamie her bracelet. And a sighting of a girl with blond hair."

"What about my T-shirt?" I asked.

"She thought someone from Kentville trashed the banner," Jessi reminded me. "She'd probably say the same thing about your shirt."

Everyone looked sad and defeated. Then Jessi's eyes lit up. "I think I know what to do."

"What?" I asked, curious as to how we could even begin to fix this, and a little nervous that Jessi had another crazy plan.

"Holly Phillips—she goes to my church and she goes to Riverdale. Plus she's on the soccer team!" Jessi said, like she had everything figured out.

"Um, okay, but how does that help us?" I wondered.

"You don't know Holly. Her mouth runs a mile a minute. She'll tell you what she ate for breakfast, but she'll also drop juicy gossip, like who is feuding with who over at Riverdale," Jessi said.

"She might talk a lot, but I don't think she'll tell you, a Kangaroo, about her team's plot to sabotage us," Emma said doubtfully.

"She wouldn't tell me, but what if she told it to another Ram?" Jessi said, her eyes gleaming.

"Still not getting it," I said.

Jessi leaned back in her chair and grinned. "We've got a lot of talent on the Kicks, and that includes a talented actress—Frida." Frida glowed at Jessi's compliment. "What if Frida pretends she's a new student and wants to join the Rams? And gets Holly to spill everything?"

"Wouldn't they know what Frida looks like?" Zoe asked.

Jessi nodded. "She'd have to wear a disguise, of course."

Frida smiled. "I could go to the Rams' practice after school tomorrow. I'll say I just moved to Riverdale and am interested in joining the soccer team."

"But you'll miss *our* practice!" I said, alarmed. After the game we'd just played, we needed to step it up!

"Chill, Devin. It's only one practice," Jessi said. "We've got to find out what else the Rams have planned. If it's something really terrible, all the practice in the world won't help us."

Jessi had a point. The sabotage had slowly and surely gotten into the Kicks' heads and messed with our performance. We needed to put a stop to it once and for all!

"Do you think you can pull it off, Frida?" I asked. "Acting onstage, or even on the soccer field, is one thing. But this is more like being a spy!"

"I can handle it," Frida said, her eyes dancing. "It's going to be fun!"

The next day at soccer practice, Jessi, Emma, Zoe, and I kept exchanging nervous glances. Frida had promised to come right over to the Kicks' field as soon as she was finished. What if she got caught?

We played a scrimmage, and Coach Flores rotated all of us between offense and defense to give everyone several shots on the goal. It was time to cool down, and Coach had us all stretching, something new she had been trying out. It reminded me a little bit of the tai chi we had done with the seniors, and I felt myself beginning to relax, when I spotted a girl I had never seen before pedaling her bike to the end of the field.

Jessi looked up too. "It's Frida!" she hissed.

"No way!" I said. But when Coach called practice, Jessi raced over to her. Zoe and Emma looked at me. I shrugged. "Let's go!"

We followed, and when I got closer, I could tell the girl indeed was Frida, but it wasn't easy!

"Wow, Frida," Emma said, impressed. "I never would have recognized you."

"I raided the prop room in the theater department this morning," Frida said as she climbed off her bike. Her curly auburn hair was hidden, replaced by two brown braids running down her back. She took off the helmet, and now we could also see her brown bangs. She was wearing a wig! Her eyes, usually swept with black dramatic eyeliner, were bare. Instead she wore glasses with thin black frames.

"You don't wear glasses. How can you see?" Jessi asked.

Frida took the glasses off and tapped the lenses. "They're prop glasses—it's clear glass!"

"So did you find anything out?" I asked eagerly.

"I sure did, and then some!" Frida said as she leaned the bike against the fence and pulled off the messenger bag she had slung across her shoulders. She reached into the bag and pulled out a mini audio recorder.

"And I've got it all recorded!" she said triumphantly.

"I'm glad Jessi showed me that picture of Holly. I was able to find her right away and start a conversation. And, boy, oh boy, did she sing like a canary!"

"Play it!" Jessi demanded.

Frida grinned and hit a button. Soon we could hear a voice saying, "Hi, I'm Diana." The voice was high-pitched and really upbeat and cheery.

"That's me," Frida mouthed. It didn't sound anything like her!

"I'm transferring here and wanted to check out the soccer team," "Diana" continued. "I was hoping I could make the team."

"We're in the middle of the season, and full up, but what grade are you in? Maybe you can play next year," a voice said in return.

"That's Holly," Frida whispered to us.

Diana and Holly chatted back and forth for a while, and Holly was telling a long story about how her social studies teacher had broken out in hives in class that day, when Frida struck.

"I really wanted to go to Pinewood," she said. "Their team is awesome, but my parents can't afford to send me there. Another team I've been hearing a lot about lately is the Kentville Kangaroos. I wouldn't mind playing for them."

"Trust me, you're way better off with the Rams," Holly answered. Her voice dropped lower. "The Kangaroos may have been doing better, but I know for a fact they are not going to make it to the play-offs."

"How could you know something like that?" Frida, as Diana, asked innocently.

There was a long pause before Holly spoke again. Her voice had gotten even lower, barely above a whisper. Huddled around the audio recorder, we all strained to hear her.

"Because it's against our league rules to play on a field that's anything but green grass," Holly confided. "If you don't have green grass or turf, you have to forfeit the game."

"The Kicks don't have a green field? That's weird," Frida said.

Holly giggled. "They do now, but they'll be in serious trouble when they spray paint 'Kangaroos Rule' in big blue letters all over the field before their next game."

"Why would they do something like that?" Frida asked.

"Maybe *they* won't. Maybe someone else will before the game on Saturday," Holly said.

"Wait, are you saying that the *Rams* are going to spray paint the Kentville field?" Frida asked. "What an awesome idea!"

"Oh my gosh!" Jessi cried, and Frida stopped the recording. "Are you serious? They're going to paint our field? That's extreme."

"Extremely nasty," Emma agreed. "Especially the part about how they'll make it look like we did it ourselves."

"This is incredible," I said, shaking my head.

"There's more," Frida said. "I only said that last thing

to butter her up so she'd keep talking. And wow, did it work." She turned the recorder back on.

"Yeah, it's the perfect plan, and it was all Jamie's idea," Holly chattered on. "Jamie is our team captain. If we spray 'Kangaroos Rule' on the school field, the one where both teams play, everyone will think the Kangaroos did it themselves. They'll be in big trouble. We're hoping it will be big enough that the Kangaroos' girls' and boys' teams will have to forfeit against us that day. Then we'll be guaranteed a slot in the play-offs."

"How would you even pull something like that off?" Frida asked.

"Jamie's got the cans of blue and white spray paint already," Holly continued, spilling all. "We're going to go to the field early Saturday morning—around eight a.m., when no one will be there yet. We'll do it then. When everyone shows up for the game, surprise!"

"Wow, that's pretty smart," Frida said.

"Jamie's really smart," Holly said. "We've already done a bunch of stuff to them. Like, she found some of the Kangaroos' e-mail addresses online and sent them a fake e-mail that looked like it was from their coach so they would all get to practice late by mistake."

"Genius," said Frida.

Then Holly started chattering on about the Rams' uniforms, and Frida shut off the recorder.

"Unbelievable!" Jessi cried, her face contorted with anger.

"Not only would we have to forfeit, but we would get in trouble for spray painting our field too!" Zoe said, outraged.

"Remember how I said I'm totally not cut out for revenge?" Emma asked angrily. "Well, I was wrong. I'd love to get some revenge on those Rams!"

I held my hands up in the air. "No more revenge! What we need to do is figure out a way to stop them."

"Could we bring the recording to the league director?" Zoe suggested. "That would have to convince anyone!"

"But then the Rams will be disqualified," I said. "And if we do make it to the play-offs, everyone will say it's only because we never had to play the Rams. I want to beat them fair and square!"

"That means we need to figure out a way to stop them from painting our field," Jessi said. "And fast!"

CHAPTER SIXTEEN

We were bouncing around some ideas about how to stop the Rams, when Jessi made a good point.

"This involves the boys' team too," she said. "We need to warn them!"

That's why the next day at lunch Jessi and I were sitting with Cody and Steven. I felt so awkward because this was the first time we were talking after I'd acted like a total dork when Steven had asked me to the carnival. When we first sat down, he didn't even look at me. I felt my cheeks get hot, but Cody and Jessi didn't notice the weirdness between us. Or if they did, they didn't let on.

"Do you remember how I tried to tell you the Panthers were trying to sabotage both of our teams?" Jessi asked.

Cody laughed. "Not this again!"

Jessi's eyes flashed angrily. "I was wrong about only one thing. It's the Rams, not the Panthers, who are sabotaging us. They've got something big planned for our games this Saturday. This time I've got undeniable proof." She plunked the audio recorder down on the table.

"What—," Steven started to say, when Jessi shushed him.

"Be quiet and listen," she said. "You're about to hear Holly, one of the Rams, talking." Jessi had fast-forwarded the recording to the part where Holly spilled everything.

She turned the recorder on, and Steven and Cody listened. Cody at first had a mocking grin on his face, but it slowly faded as he heard the details of the Rams' plan.

"Wow," Cody said, shaking his head. "I can't believe another team would try to make both of our teams forfeit."

"Did you play it for Coach Flores?" Steven asked, looking at me for the first time since I'd sat at the table.

"No," I said. "I want to beat the Rams fair and square, not because they get disqualified."

"So we have to stop them before they do it," Jessi added. "And we've got a plan. We were hoping you would help us."

The idea had been Emma's. She'd said, "What if we were waiting for them Saturday morning? As soon as they got on the field, we could turn the sprinklers on them!"

Jessi told Cody and Steven the Kicks' plan.

Cody laughed. "It would serve them right! Hey, I had a part-time job over the summer with the maintenance crew at Kentville. I used to mow the grass and stuff. I know where the shut-offs are for the sprinklers."

"Perfect!" Jessi said. "So we'll meet at the field at seven thirty a.m.?"

"Wait," Steven interrupted. "How are we going to explain to our parents why we need to be at the soccer field so early?"

Jessi shrugged. "Special training for the big soccer games that day? We'll think of something!"

"Thanks for warning us," Cody said.

"Yeah, thanks," Steven added. "It would have been the worst if we'd had to forfeit Saturday's game."

Jessi grinned. "You're welcome. Now you know I was right, so feel free to go ahead and apologize for not believing us the first time."

Cody laughed again. "Come on, Jessi. You have to admit that you sounded pretty crazy."

Oh, no, I thought. *Here we go again.* Jessi's back stiffened and the smile left her face, but Cody was totally oblivious to her body language.

"So, Jessi, are we still on for the carnival?" he asked with a smile.

"I don't think so," Jessi said primly as she stood up to leave. "Let's go, Devin," she said, and she stalked off.

I saw Cody, his eyes wide and his shoulders raised in a questioning shrug, looking at Steven.

Why does Kentville even hold this stupid carnival? I thought as I followed an angry Jessi out of the cafeteria. It was causing way too much trouble!

⚽

Between the sabotage, homework, and soccer practice, I had missed a bunch of webcam sessions with Kara. That night I made sure to keep the date. I had so much to tell her!

"Oh, so you're alive," Kara said sarcastically. "I was beginning to wonder."

"What do you mean?" I asked, surprised at the tone of her voice.

"I just haven't seen you in a while," Kara said, and she looked kind of mad.

"I know," I said. "It's just—"

"Forget it," Kara snapped, cutting me off. "Listen, I have to go. I'm *busy*. You should understand that, right?"

Before I could answer her, she vanished from the screen. I stared at it for a moment, sad. Kara was totally upset! I figured it was because I had missed those webcam sessions, but she should have understood that, right? Aren't friends supposed to understand stuff like that?

Now I was totally in a bad mood. I stomped down the stairs and into the kitchen. My dad had on the apron that Maisie and I had given him the previous Father's Day. It had yellow caution tape on the front and said, STAND BACK. DAD IS COOKING.

"What's for dinner?" I asked.

"My famous turkey burgers," he replied as he flipped one in the grill pan.

Dad's turkey burgers were famous, but when he'd first started making them, they had not been famous in a good way, if you know what I mean. Dry and tasteless, they'd been more like hockey pucks than burgers. Even my mom, who was a stickler for us cleaning our plates, had said we could throw them in the garbage! But he kept experimenting with the recipe, and now they were moist and delicious.

"Okay," I said, my voice flat.

Dad frowned. "Usually you do cartwheels for my turkey burgers. What's up, Dev?"

I didn't really feel like talking, but Dad was a good listener. So I took a deep breath. "I think Kara's kind of mad at me," I began.

Dad turned away from the stove and looked at me. "You and Kara hardly ever fight. What's going on?"

I told him how busy I had been with soccer and schoolwork and how I'd missed a bunch of our webcam sessions.

"She knows how busy I am, between soccer and school and everything," I said. "Shouldn't she be a little more understanding about it?"

Dad sat down at the kitchen table while I sat across from him.

"I'm sure she understands," he said. "But I don't blame her if she's feeling a little hurt, too. You have been a little soccer obsessed lately, Devin."

I sighed. Everyone was calling me soccer crazy!

"I just want the Kicks to make it to the play-offs!" I said.

"If the Kicks don't make the play-offs, the world won't end." Dad gave me a little smile. "Life will go on, but it may be a life without Kara if you don't start making time for her."

I shuddered. If the Kicks didn't make the play-offs, I'd really need Kara! And if the Kicks did, she'd be the first person I would want to tell.

"It's not healthy to be too focused on just one thing," he continued. "You need to make sure you take the time to be with the people who are important to you. So try to make some time for her, okay? And if you can't, then maybe you can text her. So she knows you're not just blowing her off."

I nodded. He was so right!

"Thanks, Dad!" I walked around the table and gave him a big hug. "Do I have time to call her before dinner?"

Dad smiled. "I'll keep the turkey burgers warm."

I knew I probably couldn't get Kara back on the webcam, so I called her home phone—something I hadn't done since we were kids. Her mom answered.

"Hi, Mrs. O'Connell," I said. "May I please speak to Kara?"

"Of course, Devin!" she said, and then I heard some shuffling, and Kara's muffled protests, but then she got on the phone.

"Hello," she said flatly.

"Listen, I know you're mad," I said. "And I'm sorry. Really, really, really, really sorry. I don't mean to be igsnoring you, I swear."

Kara giggled. "Did you just say 'igsnoring'?"

"Well, I meant to say 'ignoring,'" I said. "You know what I mean."

"Is that like when you ignore someone while you're snoring?" she asked.

Now I was giggling. "I am not snoring! Or ignoring! I swear. I'm just really, really, really, really sorry."

"Well, as long as you're really, really, really, really sorry, I forgive you," Kara said.

"Thank you!" I cried. "And if I can't webcam you, I promise I'll text or something. I hate you being mad at me. You're still my best friend, even if you're, like, a thousand miles away."

"Two thousand nine hundred eighty-nine point nine miles," Kara said, and I was impressed. I knew if Kara had memorized the miles between us, she had to really miss me.

"Devin! Dinnertime!" Dad called out.

"I have to go," I said. "Are we cool?"

"As long as you don't igsnore me anymore," Kara teased, giggling again.

"You are so weird!" I cried, and then I hung up the phone, and I felt really relieved that things were right between us again.

CHAPTER SEVENTEEN

"This is so exciting!" Emma whispered as we made our way across the parking lot early Saturday morning.

Frida looked around. "Any sign of the Rams yet? I keep worrying that they'll get here early."

"No, but I see Cody and Steven," Jessi said, pointing. The two boys were over by the equipment shed next to the school field.

We all jogged up to meet them.

"Hey," Cody said, nodding.

"So what's the plan?" Steven asked.

I looked at Jessi. So far she'd had a plan for everything, and she didn't disappoint.

"Here's what I'm thinking," she said. "Cody, you know where the sprinkler shut-off is, right? So you and Steven should be stationed there. We'll hide by the bleachers. As soon as the Rams are on the field, we'll text you, and then you turn the sprinklers on."

Steven took out his phone and looked at me. "Give me your number, and I'll send you a text," he said.

"Sure," I replied, and I think I blushed a little when I gave it to him. Sure, we were doing this for a serious reason, but I had never given a boy my cell number before.

"And I've got yours, Cody," Jessi said. "We'll text both of you; in case one doesn't go through, the other can be backup."

I looked at the time on my phone. "We'd better take our places. The Rams could be here any minute."

The boys headed to the back of the shed, and Emma, Zoe, Frida, Jessi, and I raced to get under the bleachers. We ducked under the metal supports and crouched down. Now we had a view of the entire field.

"I still can't believe that the Rams would actually paint our field to make us forfeit," Zoe remarked. "That is so mean."

"There are mean people in the world," Frida said solemnly.

"I don't think they're mean, exactly," Jessi said. "I think they're just obsessed with winning."

Obsessed with winning. Was I one of those people? That was basically what everyone had been saying about me lately. But I could never imagine taking it as far as the Rams had. I wanted to win because we were the best team.

Emma gasped, interrupting my thoughts. "There they are!" she hissed.

I almost couldn't believe it. Four girls carrying spray cans were walking onto the field, looking around to make sure the coast was clear. They all wore hoodies and shorts. Then one girl pulled down her hoodie, and long, blond hair spilled out.

"That's Jamie," Jessi whispered.

"Text the boys!" Emma whispered.

"Not yet," Jessi said. "The sprinklers are built-in, and yesterday I came and checked out where they are. We need to turn them on when the Rams are in range. Devin, get the message ready, and hit send when I tell you."

I clicked on Steven's number in my phone and typed "NOW." My finger hovered over the green button, ready to send.

We could see (but not hear) Jamie talking to the other girls. She started pointing to different spots on the field, and the group of them began to move toward the center.

Jessi grinned. "Now!"

We both hit send. Nothing happened for a few seconds. And then . . .

Whoosh! The sprinklers kicked on in high gear. The four Rams began to shriek as the cold water rained down on them. Confused, they started to run off the field toward the parking lot.

Jessi ducked under the railing and took off after them like a shot. Was she going to confront them? I chased after her, and Emma, Frida, and Zoe followed me.

Jessi cut the girls off before they could reach the parking lot. She stood there with her hands on her hips, grinning.

"Hi, Jamie," she said as the Rams skidded to a stop. "What are you guys doing here so early?"

Jamie's mouth dropped open as the rest of us ran up to Jessi. Behind Jamie's blue eyes you could practically see the gears of her brain whirring as she tried to think of what to say. Water dripped from her long hair, and her hoodie was soaked. The three girls with her all looked like drowned rats too.

"We were just . . . I mean . . ."

"We know what you were going to do," Jessi said.

The other girls looked terrified, and Jamie's face turned bright red. But she tried to keep up a tough act. "Oh, yeah? So what? Go ahead and tell on us."

I stepped forward. "We're not going to do that," I said. "We can settle this on the field."

Relief flickered in Jamie's eyes, but it was quickly replaced by determination. "Fine," she said.

She motioned for the Rams to follow her, and they started to walk away, but I had a question for them.

"Why us?" I called out.

Jamie turned around. "Why should I tell you?"

I thought quickly. "Well, I just might change my mind about turning you in."

Jamie scowled. "Fine," she said. "Listen, it's not personal.

Last year we came so close to winning the league. We lost two of our best players this year, and after a couple of games, it looked like we might have a hard time getting into the play-offs. Then you guys starting winning. . . . We just wanted some insurance, that's all."

Then I realized something. "Wait a second," I said. "If you guys lose to us today, you'll lose your play-off spot, won't you?"

"It's totally not fair," Jamie said, and I noticed a coldness in her blue eyes. She wasn't angry, or mean, or spiteful . . . just determined to win, no matter what it took. "We're a good team. We deserve that slot. I haven't been playing soccer since I was three to lose now."

Jessi stepped up. "We know you framed Mirabelle for it."

Jamie grinned like a snake. "Yeah, that was pretty smart, wasn't it? Everybody in the league knows how Mirabelle ditched you guys for the Panthers. It was obvious. I was hoping that the Panthers would get in trouble for it, but it doesn't matter. We'll take care of them in the play-offs."

"If you get to the play-offs," I said. "You have to beat us first."

"Right. Good luck with that," Jamie said, and her friends giggled.

"We are *not* losing today," Jessi said, her eyes flashing with anger.

Jamie shrugged. "I guess we'll find out. See you later."

The other Rams started giggling as they turned and

walked away, and I saw Jessi's mouth open. I put a hand on her shoulder.

"Leave it," I warned. "It's not worth it. We'll show them."

I took out my phone and quickly checked the online stats for our division. I was right—if the Rams lost the game against us, they would lose the play-off spot. But if we won, we'd be in!

"Beating the Rams is our best revenge," I said. "And when we do, we'll be in the play-offs!"

"Seriously?" Emma asked.

I nodded. "We're just one game away."

"And don't forget, your secret weapon is back," Zoe said. "Me! I'm cleared to play today."

"Right! I totally forgot!" I shrieked. I hugged her. "The Kicks are back!"

The sprinklers on the field turned off, and Cody and Steven jogged up to us.

"That was awesome," Cody said. "Those girls got drenched."

"Just wait till the game," I said. "We're going to wash them out with a tidal wave of teamwork!"

Jessi grinned. "That might be the dorkiest thing you've ever said. But I love it."

I smiled back. "That's because it's true!"

Tweeeeeeeeeeet!

The ref's whistle blew, and one of the Rams' midfielders raced up to the ball to make the starting kick of the game. Coach Flores had placed me, Zoe, and Megan on the forward line, and Jamie was on the Rams' forward line, facing me. With some satisfaction I saw that her hair was still damp from the sprinklers. She darted past me as the midfielder lobbed a short pass to her, and as she dribbled forward to set up a pass to another Rams striker, I made sure I stuck to her as closely as I could. Frustrated, she gave the ball a wild kick, which sent it flying out of bounds.

Getting caught by us must have gotten to Jamie, I thought, but even though I was right, the Rams still played a good game. When Zoe threw the ball from the sideline to Grace, one of the Rams midfielders swept in from out of nowhere and intercepted it. She sprinted down the right flank with the ball as Maya tried to catch up to her from the midfield. But Frida, on defense, got to her first, and stole the ball away with a short punt that landed in the middle of nowhere. The Rams and Kicks converged on it, but Jessi got to it first and shot it downfield.

Zoe jetted up to it, got control of the ball, and then did that beautiful thing she did best, zigzagging between the defenders as she made her way to the goal. I tore up to meet her, with Jamie right at my heels, but Jamie couldn't catch me.

Zoe floated a perfect pass to me right before two Rams defenders nearly collided in front of her. I stopped the ball with my foot and then followed up quickly with a kick. The world turned to slow motion as the ball sailed over the head of a Rams defender. Had I overshot it?

No. The ball whizzed past the goalie and bounced into the back of the net.

"Goal!" the ref cried, and the Kicks' fans in the stands began to cheer. I jogged back to the other end of the field, grinning as I passed Jamie.

"I guess we Kangaroos can kick after all," I told her, and she scowled at me.

That first goal set the tone for the rest of the game. The gray cloud that had hung over us when we'd played the Atoms had dissolved. Nobody was thinking about sabotage. We just played our best.

After that goal one of the Rams kicked a wild ball, and Jamie and I both went after it. As she ran past me, she pushed into me, hard, and I lost my balance.

Tweet! The ref called a yellow card on her.

"Keep doing it," I cheerfully told her. "You'll just be sitting out the rest of the game."

That comment earned me another scowl, but I let it slide off me. Jamie was not going to get under my skin—not anymore.

We scored two more times in the first half—Zoe and Megan each got a goal. Jamie scored for the Rams, so we ended the half 3–1. Coach Flores put Brianna in for me at the start of the second half, so I got to watch the game from the sideline for a little while.

The Rams came back strong in the second half, and for a little while I got worried. I realized that when they were focused, they played like a well-oiled machine, moving the ball down the field with a series of controlled, orchestrated passes. And they were fast, so it was hard for our defense to anticipate their moves. Jamie ended up making two goals in the first ten minutes of the half, tying the game at 3–3.

After Jamie's third goal, Coach Flores sent me in to sub for Megan, and replaced two of the midfielders and one defender. With fresh energy on the field, we quickly gained momentum. Jamie charged down the field, but Frida stopped her cold, sweeping in front of her and intercepting the ball. She punted it to Grace in the midfield, who took it all the way up the left side and scored.

"Hey, I forgot—what character are you playing today?" I asked Frida as we jogged back downfield.

She grinned. "Today I'm a member of the Kicks who really wants to beat the Rams."

I smiled back. "It's your best role yet!"

With time ticking on the clock, the Rams started to get desperate again. One of them—not Jamie—shoved Maya out of the way as she went for a ball. The ref threw a yellow card, but it didn't stop one of the Rams' forwards from gaining control of the ball on the next play and shooting it past Emma, who was so angry about the flag that she forgot to watch the goal. The score was tied again.

The refs threw two more yellow cards on the Rams as the half wound down, but at least they weren't scoring. We weren't having much luck either, until one of the Rams sent a crooked pass sailing over the sideline. Maya threw it back in, and Jessi was right on top of it.

She charged down the field like she was on fire, blazing past the defending midfielders.

"Whoo! Go, Jessi!" yelled the Kicks on the sideline.

Alarmed, the Rams defense all zoomed toward her, but I had been keeping a parallel course with her all the way down the field. Before the defense got to her, she floated a pass right to me, and I got it. With Jamie right on my heels, I stormed the goal and slammed the ball toward it.

Once again the ball seemed to move in slow motion. The ball kissed the inside edge of the goalpost, and the Rams' goalie made a valiant dive for it, but she couldn't get to it in time.

"Goal!"

Jessi ran up and high-fived me. The ball went back in play, but the Rams didn't get far before the ref's whistle blew. Game over!

I knew what that meant, but I looked at the scoreboard to make sure. HOME: 5. AWAY: 4.

"We made the play-offs!" I shrieked. Jessi, Zoe, Brianna, and the other Kicks slammed into me, and we started jumping up and down.

"Come on. We can't forget about the Rams," Grace announced, and we calmed down so we could line up and shake hands. The Rams all looked miserable.

I shook Jamie's hand last. "Good game," I said, trying to show some sportsmanship, but Jamie just scowled at me. As I jogged away, I had a thought. Maybe if Jamie had worried more about practicing instead of sabotaging us, her team might have gotten that play-off spot she wanted so badly.

I caught up with the rest of the team off the field, and we started cheering and hugging and screaming again.

"We did it!" I squealed, hugging Jessi.

"Because you're a great captain," Jessi said.

"And you're a great detective," I told her.

Jessi smiled. "I know."

Coach Flores raised her voice. "I'm so proud of you girls!" she said. "This means our season is extended, so I'll see you all on Monday for practice."

I was about to raise my hand and suggest that we have an extra practice tomorrow morning, but then Grace spoke up.

"The Kicks are all going to the carnival tonight!" she called out, and everyone cheered.

I had almost forgotten about the carnival. I knew it would go late, and we might be tired, and . . . then I remembered what my Dad had said, about how the play-offs weren't everything. My friends were just as important.

"You're coming, Devin, right?" Emma asked.

"Of course I am!" I replied.

CHAPTER EIGHTEEN

"How do I look?" I asked, spinning around in front of the webcam. Mom had bought me the cutest dress—Kicks blue with no sleeves, and a little white belt around the middle.

"Perfect!" Kara replied. "Blue looks nice on you. What shoes are you wearing?"

I held up my foot so she could see, and Kara laughed.

"Flip-flops? Seriously? I've already got my boots on," she said.

I heard a horn beep outside, and I knew that was Jessi and her dad.

"My ride is here," I said. "But I promise I'll chat you tomorrow morning, okay? I'll let you know everything that happens."

"Say hi to *Steven* for me," she teased, and I stuck out my tongue as I shut the laptop.

I ran downstairs and found Mom, Dad, and Maisie waiting for me by the front door.

"You look beautiful," Dad said, giving me a hug.

"Just lovely," Mom added. "Now don't forget, we want you home by ten."

Maisie rolled her eyes. "Why can't I stay up late?"

"I better not keep them waiting," I said quickly, anxious to avoid a Maisie scene. "See you later!"

I ran to the car and squeezed into the backseat with Emma and Zoe. Jessi sat in the passenger seat up front.

"Frida's meeting us there," Emma informed me.

"Cool," I said.

My friends all looked really nice. Zoe had on a white, gauzy short dress and these really cool wedge sandals. Emma wore jeans and a pink tank top, and her jeans weren't wrinkly like they usually were. I craned my head around the seat to check out Jessi, who had on skinny jeans and a gray short-sleeved top layered over a red tank top. She had these beautiful silver hoop earrings, too.

"This is such an amazing day," Emma said. "We beat the Rams, the boys beat the Rams, and now we're going to a carnival!"

"I'm glad we're all going together," I said. "Will everyone else be with, like, a date?"

"That's what I heard," Emma replied a little nervously.

"My sister Opal says that everyone says they're going with a date, but not many people do," Zoe reported, and that made me feel a little better.

We quickly reached the school, and Mr. Dukes dropped us off out front. The carnival had been set up in the teacher parking lot and the big grassy field next to it. Crowds of kids were already milling around.

"Have a nice time!" Jessi's dad said. "I'll be back for you all at around nine thirty."

It was getting dark already, but big spotlights lit up the carnival area. We lined up to pay our admission and then looked around.

There were a bunch of booths; some of them had carnival games, and a few others sold ice cream and hot dogs and popcorn and cotton candy. On the grassy part a few rides had been set up—one of those giant inflatable slides, and a spinny thing, and even a small Ferris wheel.

"Kicks!"

Frida came running toward us, followed by Brianna, Anna, Sarah, and a bunch of other girls from the team. Everyone started talking and laughing at once.

For a second I couldn't believe it. Just a few weeks before, I'd been brand-new at the school and hadn't known anyone. Now here I was, surrounded by a whole group of friends, co-captain of a soccer team headed for the play-offs. Things were looking pretty good.

Then Jessi nudged me. "Look," she said, pointing.

Cody, Steven, and some other guys from the boys' team were standing in front of one of the games. I had to admit, it was kind of a relief to see that Steven didn't have a date with him or anything.

"Should we talk to them?" I asked.

Jessi looked thoughtful for a few seconds. She walked off and bought a cone of blue cotton candy. Then she grabbed my arm.

"What are we doing?" I asked, but she didn't answer.

Jessi marched up to Cody and handed him the cotton candy. "I got this for you," she announced.

Cody took it from her. "Thanks."

Then I knew that whatever had been weird between Jessi and Cody had been settled. Now I just had to settle the weirdness between me and Steven.

"So, I'm sorry I said I didn't want to come here with you," I said, looking down at my flip-flops. "I was just really stressed about soccer and everything."

I looked up into his eyes then, and felt my cheeks get warm. Steven smiled.

"Do you guys want to go on the Ferris wheel?" he asked.

I didn't hesitate. I still wasn't sure about dating, but a Ferris wheel—that was easy.

"You bet," I replied, and the four of us walked off together.

See what the Kicks are up to next!

"Stay on your toes! You gotta be ready for the ball!" Coach Flores shouted encouragingly.

I stood across from my friend Jessi at soccer practice at Kentville Middle School, a soccer ball in my hands. I tossed the ball to her. Jessi stopped it with her upper thigh, bounced it down to her foot, and kicked it back at me. We were doing a volley exercise, passing the ball back and forth using different parts of our body.

"Keep it coming, Devin!" Jessi called out as she danced around on her feet, waiting for the ball.

I threw the ball again, and this time Jessi ducked into it, her braids flapping in the wind as she hit the ball back to me with her head.

"Now, that's using your head!" my other friend Emma called to us, laughing at her own silly joke.

"Boo!" I heard Grace, the eighth-grade captain of the

Kentville Kangaroos (otherwise known as the Kicks), call out. "That's the oldest soccer joke in the book!"

"Not the oldest," Emma said with a gleam in her eyes. "Why did Cinderella get kicked off the soccer team?"

Groans broke out over the entire soccer field before all the Kicks replied together:

"Because she ran away from the ball!"

"Now, that," Emma said, smiling triumphantly, "is the oldest soccer joke around!"

Everyone started cracking up, even Coach, who chuckled as she glanced at her wristwatch. "We might as well call it quits. I haven't had a chance to check out today's paper, and I'd like to do that while you are all still here. The article about the Kicks was supposed to run today!"

Everyone began buzzing excitedly as Coach went to her office to get the newspaper.

"Do you think my photo is in it? I hope they got my good side!" said my friend Frida. (She wanted to be an actress someday, so she was always worried about her good side.)

"I have to text my mom and make sure she picks up a paper," Zoe added.

I grinned at my friends. When I'd first joined the Kicks at the start of the school year, the team hadn't been doing so well. But now we were headed to the play-offs, and a reporter and a photographer from the *Kentville Chronicle* had showed up at a practice the week before. The reporter had asked us a bunch of questions, and then the photographer had clicked away as we'd played a scrimmage.

"We're in luck! Coach Valentine left a bunch of copies on my desk," said Coach Flores. She gave one to Frida before she moved down the field, handing out newspapers randomly to the other Kicks as she went. Jessi, Emma, and Zoe huddled around Frida, and I joined them.

"It's in the sports section, section C," Coach called.

Frida eagerly leafed through the newspaper, dropping pages onto the field until she found the article.

"Ta-da!" she cried, pointing to the team photo of the Kicks plastered across the page. "Maybe a big casting director will see me in this photo and just have to have me in her next project!" She got a faraway look in her eyes.

"Um, hello?" Jessi said impatiently as she picked up the newspaper pages Frida had scattered all over the field. She straightened up and waved the pages in front of Frida's face. "We want to read the article!"

"Yeah!" Emma cried. "This is so exciting!"

I looked over Frida's shoulder and saw my teammates' smiling faces looking back at me from the newspaper. We all wore the blue-and-white Kentville uniforms, which we had worn especially for the photographer that day. I saw myself grinning, wearing—of course—my pink headband.

"Kentville Kangaroos 'Kick' Their Way to the Play-Offs . . ." Frida began to read the article as Emma clapped her hands excitedly.

"It's been more than twenty years since the Kentville

Kangaroos earned their nickname, 'the Kicks.' Coach Maria Luisa Flores should know," Frida continued reading aloud. "She was a member of the middle school soccer team when the Kangaroos were two-time state champs in 1991 and 1992. It was during this time that the team got their nickname for the arsenal of kicks they used against their opponents. The name 'the Kicks' might have stuck, but the team's winning streak didn't. The Kicks haven't seen a play-off season since 1996. Even when Flores came back to her hometown to coach for Kentville a couple of years ago, the team continued to struggle, finishing 10–1 last season. 'I was focused on fun and making it a positive experience for the girls,' Flores said about her early years as the Kangaroos' girls' coach. 'But the girls made it very clear to me that they wanted to have fun while being serious competitors at the same time.'"

"Losing all the time was *so* not fun!" Emma interrupted, and everyone nodded their agreement. Even though it had been only a few months ago, it seemed more like a lifetime ago when our practices had been basically chaotic messes.

I shuddered. "Do you remember how disorganized everything was?"

"What about the Panthers game when I scored in our own goal?" Emma asked. "You can't get any more disorganized than that!"

Coach's emphasis on fun and fair above all else hadn't worked out too well. When she'd combined it with solid coaching skills, the Kicks had finally started improving.

Frida continued reading: "Flores's new coaching attitude, and some fresh blood, turned the team around. A talented group of seventh graders, including Connecticut transplant Devin Burke, the seventh-grade co-captain, are widely regarded as having jump-started the team this season."

"Devin Burke! I know her!" Jessi yelled, jumping up and down. "Will you sign an autograph for me?"

I blushed. "Cut it out," I said, swatting her hands away as she tried to hug me, acting like a crazed fan. I felt totally weird that the newspaper was singling me out. We were a team! Before I could say anything else, Frida kept on reading:

"'I don't know where my team would be without me,' Burke said at practice. The team is gearing up for their first play-off match against the Newton Tigers this Saturday."

Frida's voice trailed off as the quote sank in. She stopped reading and looked at me, her mouth open. Jessi, Emma, and Zoe all stared at me too, with surprised—and hurt—looks in their eyes.

"Wow, Devin," Jessi said slowly. The joking smile from a moment ago left her face.

I don't know where my team would be without me. The sentence echoed in my head, over and over. It sounded so stuck-up.

"I never said that!" I cried, feeling like I was on trial, with their angry eyes staring at me. I thought back to the day when the reporter, Cassidy Vale, had visited our team.

She had seemed really interested in talking to me, especially after finding out I was not only new to the team but new to Kentville Middle School.

"And you were made co-captain?" she had asked with a raised eyebrow.

"Yes," I'd said, nodding, but I hadn't told her that part of the reason was that nobody else in the seventh grade had wanted to be a co-captain at the time. The team's disorganization, plus the fact that mean Mirabelle had been the eighth-grade captain, had made the job less than desirable.

But I knew I'd made sure to tell her how much being on the Kicks meant to me. She must have gotten my words mixed up.

"I swear! I told the reporter, 'I don't know where I would be without my team' not 'I don't know where my team would be without me.' You've got to believe me!" I felt like I had swallowed a rock and that it was slowly turning around and around in my stomach.

Emma gave me a sympathetic smile. "What was in the newspaper, it really doesn't sound like something you would say, Devin."

"Never!" I said. "I remember telling the reporter that 'I don't know where I would be without my team,' because I really don't! I was so scared on the first day of school. Meeting you guys and joining the Kicks was the best thing that could have happened. If I hadn't, I'd probably still be hiding out in the bathroom during lunch!" I gave a little hiccup as I choked back tears.

"Hey, Devin, relax," Jessi said slowly as she put her arm around me. "It just took us by surprise, that's all. And the reason it was so shocking is because we would never expect you to say something like that, never!"

"They misquoted you!" Frida said. "It happens to actors all the time. It's part of being in the public eye."

"All I want to do is play soccer, not be in the public eye and get all misquoted and stuff!" I felt miserable.

Zoe gave me a hug. "I believe you, Devin. Don't worry about it. Anyone who knows you would know you'd never say anything like that."

I was taller than Zoe, so as I hugged her back, I looked over her short strawberry-blond hair at Jessi, Emma, and Frida. They were all smiling at me.

"Group hug!" Jessi called. Zoe and I each opened an arm, and everyone came pouring in.

"Thanks, guys," I said, hugging them tight. "I don't know where I would be without my friends, and you can quote me on that!"

After we all untangled from our group hug, Jessi smiled up at me. "Let's focus on the positive, which is that the Kicks have made it to play-offs!"

"Yes!" I pumped a fist in the air. "And we all worked together as a team to make that happen."

Zoe looked up. "My dad's here. Time to go!"

I followed her gaze to the parking lot next to the field. It was filling up with cars, as practice was supposed to be done by now. I spotted my family's white minivan.

Maisie, my little sister, called it the Marshmallow.

We walked over to the benches to grab our stuff, and as we did, I noticed the other Kicks still huddled around newspapers in groups. For a second I'd forgotten that the entire team was reading the article. What were they thinking about me?

We walked by Grace, the eighth-grade co-captain. She was talking with Anjali, Maya, and Giselle, all eighth graders. They looked up at us as we passed, giving me a dirty look. I stopped in my tracks.

"Look, guys, about the article," I began.

"Yeah, about the article," Anjali said. "Thanks for being on our team, Devin. I don't know what we'd do without you." Her voice dripped with sarcasm. Maya and Giselle giggled, but Grace just looked at me intently.

"That was a pretty rude thing to say," she said quietly.

"I didn't say it! I swear!" I felt like I was back at square one. I explained what I had really said and how I'd been misquoted.

"Okay, Devin," Grace said. But I could tell she didn't believe me.

"Are we cool?" I asked.

She nodded curtly but didn't say anything. Uh-oh. I didn't think we were cool at all. More like ice cold, actually.

As I went to catch up with my friends, I saw Alandra, Taylor, and Zarine join Grace and her friends. They were all eighth graders too. Anjali started whispering loudly, nodding in my direction from time to time. I heard the other girls whispering back to her as they shot looks at me.

I felt my shoulders slump as I walked to the parking lot. My best friends believed me, but it was pretty obvious my other teammates didn't.

TOM SAWYER *and* HUCK FINN
have their stories. Now it's time you heard the truth!

Read more about girls like you!

The Mother-Daughter Book Club
by Heather Vogel Frederick

I Wanna Be Your Shoebox
by Cristina García

The Truth About My Bat Mitzvah
by Nora Raleigh Baskin

The Teashop Girls
by Laura Schaefer

My So-Called Family
by Courtney Sheinmel

The Summer Before Boys
by Nora Raleigh Baskin

Published by Simon & Schuster Books for Young Readers
KIDS.SimonandSchuster.com

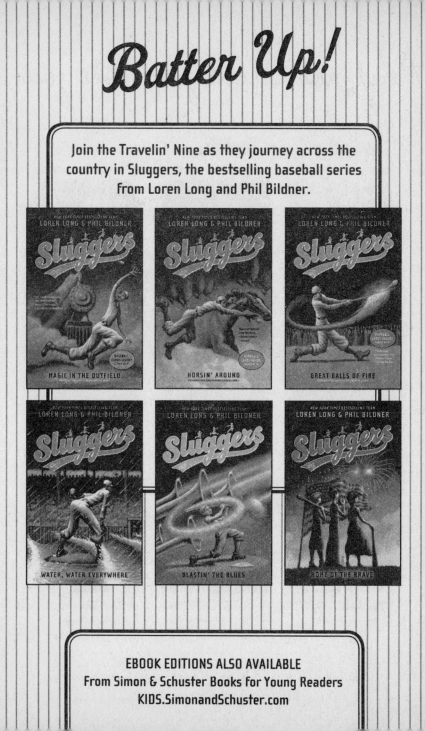